As I stood there, a crazy thought began to form in my mind. It was so wild, so completely outrageous that I hardly dared think it. Would I ever do something like that? If I only had the nerve. . . .

"Hey, slavemasters," came Danny's big voice, interrupting my daydream. "Are you going to give us orders or what?"

One by one the group drifted apart until it was just me and Kyle. Kyle was sitting on the edge of the platform, swinging his feet, relaxed and good-humored as always.

"So what's it going to be?" he asked. "Have you decided?"

"I think so," I said. I was amazingly calm. I was going to be able to go through with it.

"Okay, tell me the bad news. I have to suit up for the game soon."

"It's okay, there's no hurry," I said. "I don't need this done until after the football game."

He looked up, surprised.

"I command you to take me to the Homecoming Dance," I said, and my voice didn't even wobble.

Homecoming Dance

Janet Quin-Harkin

HarperPaperbacks
A Division of HarperCollinsPublishers

HarperPaperbacks *A Division of* HarperCollins*Publishers*
10 East 53rd Street, New York, N.Y. 10022

Produced by Daniel Weiss Associates, Inc.
33 West 17th Street, New York, New York 10011.

First printing: October, 1991

Printed in the United States of America

HarperPaperbacks and colophon are trademarks of HarperCollins*Publishers*

10 9 8 7 6 5 4 3 2 1

Chapter One

"So this is the decorations committee!" Nicole said, her voice echoing through the empty gym of Cabrillo High School, just outside San Jose, California. *Four people are going to decorate this entire place for the grad night party?* she asked herself.

She studied the three girls that had shown up: Joanie Hammond, Becky Bliese, and Gina Parducci. She knew them all, of course. As senior-class president she knew everybody. But none of them was a close friend. None of them was popular the way she was, and in the past she wouldn't have considered hanging out with any of them. Her senior year experiences had changed her thinking, but she still

1

looked at them cautiously, wondering if she would be able to work with them.

Joanie, of course, had come a long way this year, but she was still naturally shy. She was no longer the plain, dumpy girl who used to hide behind her glamorous friend Brooke. She had slimmed down and started dressing much more fashionably. She really looked pretty in her black turtleneck and white jeans. When Joanie caught Nicole looking at her she smiled nervously and looked down at her notebook.

Becky sat beside Joanie, her long straight hair hiding her face as she tried to cram in a few extra minutes of studying. Nicole secretly found Becky intimidating. Anybody who could work out complex algebraic equations in her head was not exactly normal in Nicole's opinion. Becky had always kept pretty much to herself. Nicole couldn't remember seeing her at any dances or parties. She sensed that Becky wasn't shy the way Joanie was. She just didn't bother. It occurred to Nicole that Becky could be really beautiful if she wanted. But she never wore makeup, and she usually dressed in oversize Stanford sweatshirts. Becky seemed to find ordinary people boring and juvenile. So what was she doing on a decorating committee?

Gina stood apart from the others, leaning against the gym wall, exquisitely dressed, as always, in black clothing, which accentuated her long dark lashes and heavy black hair. She was examining her fingernails. Nicole found Gina intimidating too, but for different reasons. Gina always came across as hostile, and since their big fight, she had been especially hostile to Nicole. If Nicole was surprised to find Joanie and Becky on her committee, she was astonished to see Gina there. Why would Gina Parducci want to work on *her* committee? *A blushing violet, a brain, and my worst enemy,* Nicole thought. *Kyle, I hope you appreciate this, wherever you are.*

"So it looks like it's just us," Nicole said, forcing a smile as she took her place on the bleachers beside Joanie.

"You . . . you mean no one else signed up?" Joanie asked, giving Becky a dismayed look. "Four people is a small committee."

"And how come it's all girls?" Gina demanded. "Is decorating a sexist occupation? Do they think we're going to be making paper flowers or what?"

"I don't think sexism has anything to do with it," Becky said, seriously. "I think decorating an entire gym sounds like more work than ordering food or hiring a band."

"You're right," Nicole agreed. "But we're going to need more people to help with the actual decorating. This gym ceiling is awfully high."

"We're definitely going to have it in the gym?" Gina asked.

"Well, we've got to have it at school, right? The whole class agreed that the only positive thing we could do right now for Kyle was to stop any more drunk-driving accidents. The only way to keep everyone in one place is to have the whole party at school." Nicole looked around at the expanse of white walls and ceiling, broken only by the bars on one wall and the line of pennants on another.

"The gym is so blah, though," Joanie said.

"I know, but it's the only place big enough to hold all of us," Nicole said. "It's going to take all our creativity to get this place ready for a party, but there are lots of parents who are supportive of what we're trying to do, and they'll help, too. We've got to come up with a great theme and get started with the planning."

"What kind of theme?" Joanie asked, staring up at the ceiling as if for inspiration.

Becky had been sitting, watching the others, her thoughts only partially on the discussion. Now her brain switched into high gear. Rapidly she went through possibilities until suddenly a picture of Kyle came into her head. Kyle standing out on a slippery rock at the beach, waves breaking all around him. She remembered the scene perfectly. She had yelled, frightened that he was going to be swallowed up by the water, but he had only laughed and begged her to come see the starfish in the tide pool. Kyle was another person at the seashore, excited like a little kid.

"How about an undersea fantasy?" Becky asked, her face lighting up. "That would be appropriate, wouldn't it?"

"How do you mean?" Nicole asked.

"Because Kyle loved the sea so much. He wanted to be a marine biologist," Becky said.

Becky could see the others looking at her suspiciously.

"Kyle wanted to be a marine biologist?" Nicole said, looking amused. "I never heard that before."

Becky looked at her with gray, serious eyes. "Oh, yes. He told me all about it after I started tutoring him in math."

"He was putting you on," Nicole said, still smiling. "He was great at teasing people."

"Oh, no, I'm sure he meant it," Becky said.

"It's true," Gina said, stepping forward to join the group. She had been watching the others, unsure of herself in this group, telling herself over and over to get out before she committed herself to anything. But now she couldn't keep quiet any longer. One of the most exciting moments of her life had been shared with Kyle at the beach, and it was great to be able to score a point against Nicole for once.

"He wants to study it in college. I mean . . . he wanted to study it. . . ."

Nicole was shaking her head. "I thought I knew Kyle better than most people, but I never knew he liked marine biology."

"He especially loved whales," Gina said.

"He was fascinated by whale songs," Becky added. "He asked me to find him books on whales at the Sunnyvale library." She smiled at a sudden memory. "He claimed he had never learned to find his way around libraries!"

Gina was nodding. "He liked to keep up this image of a real goof-off, didn't he? He hated people to know that he was really smart."

"I can't get over this," Nicole said.

"I only found out when we worked together as lifeguards. We saved a whale together once," Gina said.

"You were a lifeguard? I thought you worked at that clothing store," Joanie said.

"I quit that job a while ago," Gina said, making a face. "They were the pits to work for. I've been lifeguarding all spring."

"And you like that better?" Joanie asked.

"It's okay," Gina said. "It's kind of hard, now that Kyle's not . . . Her voice trailed into silence, and she stared down at her fingernails again. *I'll never forgive myself if I cry in front of these people,* she thought. *Nicole thinks she's the only one who's got a right to be upset about Kyle. She thinks she's the only one who meant anything to him. I bet she thinks Kyle only took me to the Senior Ball to be nice to me. She'll never know the truth. . . .* It took all of her concentration to stop a tear that threatened to appear on her eyelid.

Joanie toyed with the spiral back of her notebook. "I guess Kyle was really good at hiding his real self from people," she said softly. "My impression of him changed totally when I got to know him. At the beginning of senior year I thought he was some sort of god. He was so good-looking! He always seemed to be laughing, he always seemed to be at the center of things—scoring the winning touchdown, running the class meeting—always in charge of everything. Then when I got to know him, I found out that he wasn't always as sure of himself as he seemed."

Nicole nodded. "That's true," she said. "I'd been his friend all through high school and I only found out by accident that he was having problems with alcohol."

"It's funny that we all saw a different side of him," Becky said. "I know I had a bad impression of him until I got to know him. But he was really so sweet . . ."

"And fun," Joanie chimed in. "He was such fun."

"I guess it's hard for all of us to talk about Kyle," Becky said, watching Gina's face. "We're all hurting."

Nicole looked up. "I never realized any of you were that close to Kyle!" she said. Her voice and face said clearly what she was thinking—that none of them had a right to be sad about Kyle. None of them was close to him the way she was!

"You weren't his only friend in the world, you know!" Gina said sharply. "Other people are allowed to be upset, too!"

Nicole flushed. "I'm sorry," she said. "I didn't mean . . ."

"It's okay," Becky said gruffly. "None of us knew him for as long as you did. I only got to know him in the last few weeks. Until then I'd never wanted to know him better. I thought he was the exact opposite of any boy I'd ever be interested in, or who'd ever be interested in me. We were planning some great stuff to do at graduation." She paused. "Now we'll never . . ." She put her hands up and covered her face.

Joanie had been looking from one face to the next, her own throat threatening to choke up at any moment. It had been hard enough for her to volunteer for a committee; she hadn't expected to end up

8

talking about Kyle. She could see him so clearly: laughing, always laughing, doing everything at double speed, driving too fast, dancing until he dropped. She knew just what the others were feeling because she felt it, too. She put an arm around Becky.

"It's okay to cry, Becky," she said. "I wish I could cry."

"Why can't you?" Gina asked.

Joanie shook her head. "I can't feel anything anymore. I couldn't believe it when Kyle and I first became friends, and I can't believe it now that he's gone. This whole year has been totally unreal for me—like a fairy tale with an unhappy ending."

Her face was flushed and her eyes were extra bright.

"Do you want to tell us about it?" Nicole asked gently.

Joanie shook her head. "It's okay," she said. "We've got other things to do."

"Sometimes it really helps to talk about it, Joanie," Becky said, putting a hand on Joanie's shoulder. "It's a good way to handle grief."

Joanie looked embarrassed. "I wouldn't know where to start," she said.

"You could start with Homecoming," Nicole suggested.

Joanie thought for a while. "Yes," she said. "I

guess it all started with Homecoming." Joanie shifted uncomfortably in her seat, conscious of three pairs of eyes on her.

"I guess you all know about Homecoming," she said softly. "I'm sure the story got all around the school. You probably thought I was pretty dumb, but you can have no idea what it did for me— actually what Kyle did for me.

"You're probably thinking that there never was anything between me and Kyle, except for my huge crush on him. But there was something between us —after Homecoming, I mean."

She folded her hands together and gazed past the girls, images of that Homecoming dance so real and fresh in her mind that she was no longer conscious of the faces watching her. She was back with Kyle, and he was holding her tightly in his arms, laughing, always laughing. Joanie began to smile, too. . . .

Chapter
Two

I'd dreamed about him since I first saw him in our freshman year. I remember on the first day of school, he was the only person who asked a question at orientation. The principal finished her welcoming address and then said, "Are there any questions?" There was a moment's pause, and then this voice, from the back of the auditorium, asked, loud and clear, "Does the cafeteria here serve doughnuts at recess?"

The whole freshman class fell apart. I could tell the principal didn't know whether to take this as a legitimate question or a joke. Her face was radish-colored, anyway. Everyone was turning around, trying to see who had asked the question. Those who had been at junior high with Kyle knew who it was right away, and someone pointed him out. That was my first glimpse of Kyle Carpenter. He was laughing. His dark curls went every which way, and his eyes really sparkled.

I thought I'd never seen anybody as gorgeous. Neither had half the freshman class, of course. That is, all the female members. Rumors about him flew around all day: the terrible tricks Kyle had played on his teachers, the way he had put super glue in the lock of his junior high principal's office, then sounded the fire alarm. It seemed as if Kyle took nothing seriously and never even kept a girlfriend for more than a couple of weeks. I felt hopeful when I heard that. I figured that by senior year, he'd have worked his way through the entire class and would end up with me.

But by the beginning of senior year, I hadn't made much progress in getting to know him. I don't think he would have recognized me in the street. Unless I was with Brooke, of course. That's the only way I was known around school: Brooke's friend. If ever anyone talked to me that was the first thing they'd say: "Aren't you Brooke Stevenson's friend?" I'm sure nobody ever said to her, "Aren't you Joanie's friend?" I had been assigned the role of sidekick for years.

I suppose that was understandable, wasn't it? After all, Brooke was pretty and popular and smart, and I was just good old dependable Joanie: too fat, too shy, and nobody special. At least, that's how everybody thought of me until this year. The trouble was, I was really two people. The person inside of me would think of witty and clever things to say, but the person on the outside wouldn't let my lungs take in enough air to get them out.

Just listen to me talk now, and you'll realize how far I've come in a year. I would never have talked like this to almost strangers. I don't even think I told Brooke how I was feeling—really feeling inside, I mean. Of course, she wasn't too good about opening up to me, either. We kept a lot shut away from each other, which best friends shouldn't do.

Anyway, by knowing Brooke, I got closer to Kyle than I ever would have otherwise. Brooke was part of the popular group from the very beginning, and I was sometimes allowed to tag along. From the time we met in kindergarten right on through the eighth grade, that was how it worked. Brooke would be invited somewhere, and she'd bring me along. I'd always gone everywhere with Brooke—until high school. It was a shock when I realized that I might not be such a big part of her life anymore.

I remember the exact day that I first seriously thought about me and Brooke. It was after a freshman volleyball game. We'd been in high school three weeks. We were both on the freshman team: Brooke one of the star players, of course, with me doing a lot of bench-warming. We'd just won a close game and were jumping up and down, screaming and hugging each other, when a group of freshmen guys came up to us. They'd just come in from football practice and had cheered for us during the last minutes of the game. You probably remember it, right Nicole? You were one of the stars too, and it seemed as if all the guys already knew you. Pretty soon they were all talking to Brooke, too. Kyle was there, and Danny and Paul.

I remember standing at the back of the group, watching Brooke and Nicole laughing and flirting with those guys and wishing I knew the magic words to make me like them. Then one of them—it must have been Kyle because he was always the leader—said, "We're going for pizza after we've changed. You want to come?" The question was clearly directed to Nicole and Brooke and nobody else. Nicole looked at Brooke and Brooke looked at Nicole and they said "Sure" at the same time.

I waited for Brooke to say, "Is Joanie invited, too?" or "You mean we're all invited?" or something like that, the way she usually did, but she didn't say anything more.

14

"See you in a few minutes, then," Kyle said, picking up his helmet from the bench.

"A few minutes?" Danny yelled in his big voice. "A couple of hours, you mean! You know how long it takes girls to get changed?"

"I like that, Danny Russo," Nicole shouted back. "I've seen how long it takes you guys to get out of the locker room! Of course, it probably takes you a half hour to read Hot and Cold in the shower."

She and Brooke grinned at each other.

"If it takes us a long time, it's because we're exchanging stories of our latest conquests," Kyle said smoothly.

"Oh, you're into fiction?" Brooke asked. She squeezed Nicole's arm as they started to head for the locker room.

The rest of our team followed Brooke and Nicole into the locker room, everyone talking excitedly except for me. It was only as Brooke came out of the shower, her hair wrapped in a towel, that she noticed me.

"Great game, wasn't it?" she asked, her face still flushed.

"Sure," I said.

"I love high school, don't you?" she asked. "We never had guys come and cheer for our games in junior high."

"So you're going out for pizza?" I asked, trying to keep my voice steady.

She got my meaning right away. "Oh . . . gee, I'm sorry, Joanie," she said.

"That's okay. I'll see you tomorrow," I said.

Brooke looked uncomfortable. "Look, Joanie, I couldn't very well ask total strangers if you could come along, too. I mean, I thought they were only asking Nicole to begin with. I never dreamed I was included until that guy Kyle smiled at me. Isn't he a total babe? Maybe I'll get to be friends with them tonight and you can be included too, as my friend."

"Sure," I said. I stuffed things into my bag. "I'll see you tomorrow," I said. "I'd better get going. I don't like walking home alone in the dark."

"I'll call you tonight," Brooke yelled after me. "I have to tell you all about Kyle and the guys right away. I'll burst if I don't talk to you till morning."

I wanted to say that I had a lot of homework and I'd be busy all evening, but I swallowed back the words. After all, there was no sense in spoiling Brooke's evening just because I was mad. So I mumbled, "Okay, talk to you later."

On the way home it was as if a curtain had been lifted from my eyes and I could see clearly for the first time. I asked myself a lot of questions. Were four whole years of high school going to be like this? Was the only excitement in my life going to be watching Brooke go on dates with gorgeous guys and listening to the details afterward? Somehow it just wasn't enough anymore.

"I deserve a life of my own," I muttered to myself as I kicked open our gate. "And if Brooke doesn't need me for a best friend, I don't need her!"

The phone rang right after dinner and it was Brooke. "I just had to tell you all about it the moment I got home," she said. "Those guys are such fun, Joanie! That Kyle Carpenter—he tells the best stories! He nearly got kicked out of junior high school three times!"

She went on talking and talking, telling me every little thing that Kyle had done or said, and then finally, when she had to pause for breath, she said casually, "They asked me to go to their football game on Saturday, and I told them that I always did stuff with you on Saturdays, so they said I could bring you along too if I wanted."

"Look, Brooke," I cut in. "You can do stuff with them if you want to. You're not chained to me or anything."

"Are you kidding?" she asked. "I'm not going to ditch you just because we're in high school and making new friends. Of course I want you along, dummy! These guys are great. You're going to love them!"

When she hung up I had completely forgiven

her, and I was as excited about Saturday as she was. Brooke had that effect on people. You could never stay mad at her for more than a few seconds. But deep down inside me, a little seed of anger had been planted. I knew I shouldn't be angry that all the good things happened to Brooke and never to me, but I was. I told myself that I was lucky to have her as a friend, but it didn't do any good. I still felt angry. "Some day," I muttered to myself.

You're probably wondering how Brooke and I ever got to be best friends since we're so different. Believe me, I've asked myself a hundred times, over the years, why she chose me as a friend. Like I said, it all started in kindergarten.

Until Brooke got there, I hated kindergarten. I was horribly shy. It took me three weeks before I'd answer the teacher with anything but a nod. My teacher, Mrs. Rosen, was not what you would call super understanding. She even asked my mother if I knew how to talk. "Cat got your tongue?" she used to ask me, and all the other kids would laugh. They'd tease me out in the schoolyard. "Cat got your tongue?" they'd yell.

Then, after a month of school, when I had made up my mind to run away and live on berries in the forest for the rest of my life, Brooke arrived. She was so pretty, even then. She had beautiful bouncy blond curls that went up and down like springs as she moved and big, wide, blue eyes. That first time I saw her, she was wearing a pretty blue dress with a white lace collar. As she stood at the classroom door, holding her mother's hand, everybody stopped and stared at her. She looked to me just like a princess from a fairy tale. I would have hidden behind my mother's skirt with all those eyes looking at me, but Brooke didn't even blush. Instead she smiled as if we were all her long-lost friends, and I saw that she had two dimples.

I didn't think she'd ever notice me. I wasn't the type whom other people noticed, even back then. My two older sisters, Tina and Jackie, were great at all the things I couldn't do, like gymnastics and violin. While I was chubby and plain, they were skinny and pretty. I wasn't a great athlete or even a great student. And I wasn't exactly overflowing with self-confidence, even in those days.

Of course everyone in the class wanted to sit next to Brooke and be her friend. I expected that she'd make friends with Jamie Hauer and Cindy Patterson, who were the two big shots in the class.

Mrs. Rosen pulled up an extra chair to my table. "Come and sit here for the moment, Brooke," she said. "We're in the middle of writing."

"Put her next to me, Mrs. Rosen," Jamie Hauer said loudly.

"It doesn't matter where she sits right now,

Jamie," Mrs. Rosen said firmly. "Get on with your letter *A* s. I want a line of nice pointy rooftops, no wobbles."

I wanted Brooke's chair next to mine, but Mrs. Rosen slid it in on the other side of the table. As Brooke sat down she gave me a smile which made me feel warm inside.

Maybe she's a magic fairy sent to grant me three wishes, I thought. I decided right then what I would ask for: to be pretty, to have friends, and then, daringly, to have Brooke for a best friend!

"Are you with us, Joanie Hammond?" Mrs. Rosen's harsh voice brought me back to reality. "It's not nap time yet, you know."

The other kids laughed.

"You've only done three letter *A* s," Mrs. Rosen went on accusingly. "And everyone else at your table has finished. You'd better stay and finish yours while the others go out to recess."

"I haven't finished mine either," Brooke said, looking at Mrs. Rosen with those wide blue eyes. "Maybe I'd better stay in, too."

"But you just got here, honey," Mrs. Rosen said in the gentle voice she reserved for kids she liked. "You don't have to stay in and miss your recess."

"I'll finish my line with Joanie," Brooke said evenly and made her next letter *A* with determination. I noticed that when she worked, she stuck her tongue out of one corner of her mouth. I thought that was the cutest thing I had ever seen and copied her instantly.

"Oh, you stick your tongue out when you're trying hard to do something, too," she said. "Everyone teases me about it but it really helps, doesn't it? I always mess up if I don't stick my tongue out."

I opened my mouth and heard myself say, "Me, too!"

We grinned at each other in a shared secret. I was delighted and amazed that I had actually managed to talk to Brooke in a normal voice and especially amazed that Brooke was actually looking at me as if she liked me. When we had finished our line of *A*s Brooke got up. "Come on, let's go out to recess," she said. "You can show me the playground." And she took my hand and I skipped out beside her.

It was fantastic. We climbed to the top of the jungle gym together and both admitted that we were scared to let go. When we had safely reached the ground again, we sat on a bench together and traded snacks. I gave her a homemade oatmeal-raisin cookie, and she gave me some of her grapes. As we talked we discovered we both liked *Speed Racer* and *Mr. Rogers*. When the bell rang for the end of recess we were friends.

After that day, my whole world changed. Other kids stopped teasing me and started talking to me because I was Brooke's friend. I sailed through elementary school. I went to sleepovers and parties. I hardly ever asked if it was right that we always did what Brooke wanted. I just felt lucky to have a best friend who was so pretty and smart and popular.

I don't think I ever really understood why Brooke had chosen me as a friend until this year, after we'd had our big fight and all that stuff had happened with Kyle.

Chapter
Three

Over the years I had a thousand good resolutions about getting over my shyness and becoming my own person, but none of them seemed to work. My shyness lasted through elementary school, middle school, and the first three years of high school. I bet I would have gone through my whole senior year without anybody noticing I existed if a miracle hadn't happened the summer before.

Brooke had a really great job lined up. It was with a big charitable foundation, working at their headquarters. Her father had found it for her. "Just think, Joanie," she had said when she called to tell me. "I'll be handing out grants to needy people, helping to start shelters, all that sort of good stuff. My dad thinks it will look great on college applications. The only thing is," she went on hesitantly, "it's up in San Francisco and it's full-time, so I'm afraid I'm not going to have much time to do anything else this summer."

"They don't have room for one more employee, do they?" I asked. "I still don't have a job."

"Gee, I'm sorry, Joanie, I really wish you could work with me. It would be so much fun. But my dad had to pull so many strings just to get me in I don't think they'd take anyone else. They don't normally take high school kids in the summer. I'm sure there are plenty of jobs around."

Sure there are, I thought. *Brooke will be saving the world, and I'll be serving Big Macs!*

But then the first miracle happened. My sisters, Tina and Jackie, had both graduated from high school and moved away from home. Although I used to fight with them and envy them when we were little, now I missed them, especially Jackie, who was only two years older than me. She was at school at UCLA and had decided to stay in her apartment in Los Angeles for the summer. At the time, I thought this was the last straw.

"You can't do this to me, Jackie," I wailed on the phone. "I'll be all alone here. I haven't found a job yet, and Mom and Dad think I should do housework here rather than look for an outside job. Imagine being stuck in this house scrubbing and ironing all summer without you to fight with!"

I heard her laugh on the other end of the phone line.

"I'm sorry," Jackie said, "but I have to pay for this apartment year-round anyway, and it's much easier to get jobs down here. If I came home I'd have to be a waitress or a lifeguard or something else totally juvenile and miserable like that. But get a load of this and turn green! I'm going to be working at Universal Studios, helping with studio tours."

"Wow!" I said, genuinely impressed. "You're going to be one of those guides on the tour buses?"

"Not exactly," she said. "I'm going to be taking tickets at the gate, but it's almost as good."

"It sounds wonderful." I sighed.

There was a pause, then Jackie said casually, "You know, you could always come down and stay with me for the summer. Jobs really are easy to find down here, and my roommate's away until September. I might even be able to get you a job at Universal with me."

"You're kidding!" I yelled, probably blasting the phone out of her hand.

A few days later Jackie called back. She actually had been able to get me the job! My luck was beginning to change. But there was still the problem of my parents. I didn't think they would let me go. As it turned out they thought it was a great idea. "You'll be able to keep an eye on your sister," Dad said. "I didn't like the idea of her living alone for three months. You know what she's like."

"And you always were our sensible one," Mom said, beaming at me as if she'd just paid me a compliment. "We know you won't get into any crazy stuff down there, and you won't let Jackie, either!"

So that's why I was allowed to go down to L.A. for the summer—Joanie the good influence, sent to spoil my sister's wild life. Somehow I did not find this flattering. It summed up what everybody thought about me—good old reliable Joanie. You can trust her never to do anything different or outrageous or even exciting.

But of course, I didn't really care *why* they were letting me go. I was free! I was going to live in an apartment in L.A. with Jackie. There would be no curfews and nobody to tell me to finish my broccoli! I couldn't wait.

I thought Brooke would be happy for me, too. I waited until I was having dinner with her family that night to make my announcement.

"Guess what! I've found a job," I said as I spooned angel-hair pasta onto my plate.

"That's great, Joanie," Brooke said. "That day-care one you applied for?"

"Not even close," I said. "I'm going to be working at Universal Studios."

"You're kidding!" Brooke looked startled.

"But that's in Los Angeles," Brooke's mother said.

"I'm going to be living with my sister Jackie. She's got an apartment there."

"You're going to L.A. for the summer?" Brooke burst out. "Joanie, you can't do this to me! What am I going to do without you all summer?"

"You told me you'd be so busy you wouldn't have time for me anyway," I said.

Brooke had turned pale. "But I didn't think you were going to desert me," she said.

"Hey, I've got an idea. Why don't you come, too?" I asked.

"Brooke already has a prestigious job lined up," her father said calmly but firmly.

"And don't forget the SAT course," her mother added.

Brooke raised her eyebrows as she looked at me. "They've signed me up for an SAT course," she said. "All summer."

"A very expensive SAT course," Brooke's father said.

"And you definitely need it, honey," her mother added. "Remember, those PSAT scores were not

27

what we'd hoped for, were they? We're not going to get to Harvard with average test scores."

"Why do you always talk as though you're coming to college with me?" Brooke demanded. She pushed her plate away. "I'm not hungry. I'll just get an apple," she said.

A week later Brooke and I were saying good-bye. "Have a good summer, Ms. Executive Secretary," I said.

"Sure, why not?" Brooke said, her eyes extra bright. "I'll type you a memo from time to time, if you haven't been eaten by King Kong."

Summer with Jackie was all it promised to be. I loved my job in the gift shop at Universal Studios. Now that we were no longer at home, living under our parents' rules and rivals for their attention, Jackie treated me like an adult and, better still, like a friend. She'd ask my advice on what to wear on dates. We gasped together at the outrageous outfits and $2,000 sweaters when we went window shopping on Rodeo Drive in Beverly Hills. We laughed together as we tried out cooking experiments that usually became cooking disasters.

During those first couple of weeks we talked endlessly and really got to know each other for the first time. I found out how much she had suffered under our parents' strict rules. I found out that she had hated gymnastics and the violin but never dared tell anybody. That was a real eye-opener for me. I had thought that my sisters had sailed through life and that I was the only one with problems.

Armed with this knowledge, I told Jackie all about Brooke and the discoveries I had made at high school and how I had had enough of being a fly on the wall. "But I don't know how to change things," I blurted out to her.

Jackie looked me up and down. "First of all, you need a new image," she said. "I mean, who's going to look at you when Brooke is so completely gorgeous."

"That's the problem," I said, running my fingers through my hair. "Look at me. I'm totally blah."

"You need a giant dose of self-confidence," Jackie said.

"I know," I said. "I'm still shy, I guess."

Jackie examined me critically. "You need to lose weight, get a new hairstyle, improve your posture, clear up your complexion, learn to put on makeup, get a new wardrobe . . ."

"And then I might look okay?" I asked sarcastically.

"Right," she said with a laugh. "I'll make it my mission for the summer: a new, improved Joanie Hammond. Step number one is to lose fifteen pounds."

Fifteen pounds! I thought I'd die before I even began. But it wasn't nearly as hard as I'd imagined, or as hard as it would have been at home. At home my parents made things like fried chicken, hamburgers, meat loaf, and potatoes whipped up with butter. With a diet like that I was doomed, Jackie said. After a couple of weeks of salads and non-fat frozen yogurt I really did begin to notice the difference.

As soon as I'd lost most of the weight, we went shopping, and I splurged one whole paycheck on a new wardrobe.

Meanwhile, Jackie was working on my self-confidence.

"Listen up. Jackie Hammond's four-step plan for party success," Jackie said one morning in preparation for a college party she was taking me to that night. She had me practice asking the kind of questions that get people talking. "Everybody likes to talk about themselves," she told me. "Just get them started, and they'll think you are terrific!"

I tried it and it worked. I'd rehearsed my questions so well that they came out without a stutter. And once I started talking to people, I found that I could actually make some of those witty comments I always thought up but never dared say. My ultimate triumph was when a guy at a party said, "Hey, you're funny. Are you taking screenwriting at UCLA?"

On the plane back home from my wonderful summer, I let my mind play through a beautiful daydream. It was the first day of school and Brooke and I walked to school together. As we came in up the steps all the popular kids were standing together —you were there, Nicole, and Danny, Paul, and, of course, Kyle, looking tanned and gorgeous. They'd look up and, for once, their eyes wouldn't be on Brooke, they'd be on me.

"Joanie? Is that really you?"

"I can't believe it, you look so great! Were you in Paris for the summer? Those clothes!"

"Beverly Hills, dahling," I'd say and get a general laugh.

Then I'd notice Kyle. He'd be looking at me, his ordinarily sparkling eyes now smoldering. "Hey, Joanie," he'd say. "Let's compare schedules and see what classes we have together!"

And everything would progress very nicely and naturally from there. I couldn't progress it too far, because I'd never had a real boyfriend, so I wasn't totally sure what would happen.

With Kyle and me together, I saw myself doing all the things that popular, successful, and creative seniors did. I'd volunteer to be a writer for the annual one-act play contest. I'd even write articles for the newspaper this year.

I drove to Brooke's house almost the moment I got home.

"Ta-da!" I said when she opened the door.

"Joanie?" she asked.

"This is Ms. Joan Marie Hammond of Beverly Hills. How do you do," I said.

She just stared.

"So what do you think?" I asked.

"You look so . . . so different," she stammered.

"It's the new, improved Joanie Hammond," I said, turning around so that she could see me from all angles. "I've had the best summer, Brooke! How was your job? I couldn't tell much from your post-cards."

"I was so busy," Brooke said over her shoulder as we went into her house. "I didn't have time to write, with the SAT course, the job, and the commute."

"Did you give away lots of money to deserving people?" I asked.

"Oh, yes," she said breathlessly. "Lots of it."

"Boy, I bet that made you feel good."

"Right," she said.

"I've been feeling so great," I went on, not noticing at the time that for once I was doing the talking, and Brooke was strangely quiet. "My sister took me to all these incredible parties with her. Believe it or not this guy, Roger, at her apartment complex actually asked me out. He was a college sophomore! Isn't that amazing?"

"That reminds me," Brooke said, flinging herself down onto the sofa. "I didn't write to you about Damien, did I?"

"Damien?"

"This guy I worked with. He's a junior at Georgetown and he's gorgeous!"

"His name's Damien?" I said, laughing, "You better watch out. Sounds like he could be an evil spirit."

"He was wonderful," she said. "He writes poetry and he promised to write me long letters. It's perfect because I don't think I'll have time for a boyfriend at school this year."

She made it sound as if a boyfriend was an extra-curricular activity that she wasn't going to sign up for.

"All the more boys for me," I said with a laugh. "Brooke! I lost fifteen pounds, can you believe that? And I've bought lots of new clothes. I'm going to make the entire senior class notice me."

Brooke sat up suddenly. "You're not planning to wear that to school, are you?" she asked, gesturing at my miniskirt.

"What's wrong with it?" I asked.

"Maybe it's fine for L.A.," she said carefully, "but I'd be careful about wearing it here, Joanie. It might give the wrong message."

"Like what?"

She shrugged her shoulders expressively as if she wished she hadn't started the conversation.

I went home and looked at myself in the mirror again. Maybe I didn't look as good as I had thought. Maybe my clothes weren't right for Sunnyvale. My newfound self-confidence was already starting to crumble. I hadn't realized how much Brooke was at the center of my world and how much what she said mattered to me. It didn't occur to me then that she could be feeling threatened.

Chapter
Four

My grand entrance on the first day of senior year didn't go as well as I'd hoped. It wasn't that people didn't notice me. They did. I saw eyes open wide in surprise, and people said, "Wow, Joanie! You look great! You've lost so much weight!" But Kyle didn't fling himself at my feet. I wasn't catapulted into instant popularity and happiness. It was as if I'd already been given a role to play at Cabrillo High— the role of best friend to the heroine and all-round nice kid—nobody special enough to be noticed for herself.

Maybe a person can't become instantly popular just because they look better, I thought. *Maybe I'll just have to go out and do something spectacular to make them notice me.*

"I've been thinking of volunteering to write the one-act play for the festival," I said to Brooke as we sat down in English class that first day. "Do you want to do it with me?"

She shook her head. "I don't think so, Joanie. That sounds like a lot of work, and I'm already snowed under. I don't know how I'm going to do all my extracurriculars and keep up my grades, too."

"I guess we all feel like that at the moment," I said.

"I don't see why you feel stressed," she said shortly. "You've only got yearbook, and that's not too demanding. I let myself be talked into being president of half the clubs in school!"

"Then let a few things go," I said.

"But colleges look for students who are involved," she said, frowning at me. "I've got to have a whole lot going for me to get into Harvard."

"You're not seriously applying to Harvard?" I was, frankly, astounded. I mean, Brooke was a good student, but not . . . well . . .

Joanie broke off and looked around at the three faces listening intently to her story. Her gaze settled on Becky. "Well, not like you, Becky."

* * *

Anyway, I remember Brooke made a face when I blurted it out like that. "My parents want me to go," she said.

"You don't have to do what your parents want," I said. "It's your choice."

"Try telling that to my parents," she muttered. "They've already told their friends I'm going. They've probably even had announcements printed. I bet they've even bought a Harvard pennant to put up in my room."

Miss Lieberman arrived at that moment, and English class started. My mind was everywhere but on English until the end of class when she said something that immediately caught my attention.

"So, Kyle and Paul, are you still on for the one-act festival?" Miss Lieberman asked. She turned to the class. "For any of you that don't know, there is a festival of student-written one-act plays in this district every year. Paul and Kyle very bravely volunteered to write the play last summer. How's it coming along?"

"We've got the basic story," Paul said.

"Now all we need to do is write it," Kyle added, and the class laughed.

My cheeks were bright pink, and I glared at the teacher in amazement. *It's not fair!* I thought. *They didn't give anyone else a chance. It's always the*

same people who get to do everything at this school.
Nobody asked me if I wanted to try out.

Brooke gave me a commiserating smile, but I couldn't smile back.

The second big disappointment of that day happened at lunchtime. Since kindergarten Brooke and I had eaten lunch together every day. We'd always met at her locker, so naturally I went straight there after morning classes. I took out my lunch bag and I waited. The sourdough roll stuffed with turkey breast, lettuce, and mayonnaise was calling out to me, but I kept the bag firmly closed and watched for Brooke to come around the corner. The hallways emptied and still she didn't come. I was getting hungrier by the minute, but we have a "no eating in the hallways" policy at Cabrillo. After what seemed like hours I did a quick tour of our favorite eating spots, but she wasn't at any of them. Nobody I asked had seen her, and I began to get worried. Maybe something was wrong; maybe she hadn't felt well and had to go home.

I snatched a hurried bite of my roll and was on my way to the office when I bumped into her, coming down the hall with an armful of books.

"Where have you been? I've been looking all over for you," I said.

She blushed and tossed back her hair. "Sorry. I had some stuff to do in the library," she said.

"You could have told me first. I wasted most of my lunch hour standing like an idiot by your locker."

"Look Joanie," she said, "we aren't little kids any more. The world doesn't fall apart if we don't eat lunch together. You're going to have to learn to get along without me around all the time."

"Don't worry," I said frostily. "I can find plenty of people to eat lunch with. It's just that I like to be told in advance so that I don't waste a whole lunch hour waiting for someone who doesn't bother to show."

I think this surprised her. "I guess I should have warned you," she said. "It's just that I'm going to have to work my tail off this year if I have any hope of getting into Harvard, so I have a feeling I'm going to be practically living in the library."

"You need a break," I said. "And you have to eat."

"Look, I don't need you on my case, too. My parents are enough," she said.

"Fine," I said. "So now I know. I'll make other plans for my lunch hours."

"I'm sure I'll manage to get away now and then," she said.

"Let me know in advance. Have my secretary check my calendar," I said.

We stood and glared at each other. In the past a

remark like that would have made her laugh, but it didn't today. She just tossed her head and stalked off.

I found myself wondering whether she really was snowed under with schoolwork or whether she didn't want to eat lunch with me anymore. The incident made me realize that there had been a certain distance between us since I got back from L.A. I couldn't see why she'd want to avoid me. I couldn't think of anything I might have done to make her mad at me. I hadn't changed, had I?

It never crossed my mind that Brooke could actually feel threatened by me, not even the day we fought over the homecoming dress. Homecoming is a big thing at our school, and Brooke had just found out she had been nominated as a princess. I had just found out that I wasn't. Not that I really expected to be, but I had held a secret fantasy that my new, improved image might have made the difference.

"I'm so excited, Joanie," she said in the car on the way to the mall. "I've got to find the most gorgeous dress in the world. I really need your expert advice. I'm relieved, too. Now I don't have to worry about a date. A prince will have to escort me. I was really worrying about who was going to ask me. That's the problem with having a boyfriend so far away. Wouldn't it be wonderful if I was voted

Homecoming Queen? Is that something that sounds good on an application?"

"I don't think Harvard would fall over backwards about it," I said dryly.

She gave me a brief, sideways look, then shrugged. "I think I have a really good chance," she said. "There's Nicole, of course. I'm sure she has a good chance, too, but the others aren't much of a threat. Christina's a jock, Alison's too serious, and Amy's not that well-known. Nicole has more going for her on paper, I suppose. After all, she is senior-class president. I was so dumb not to run for that!"

"You just said you were doing way too much already," I reminded her. "Senior-class president is a big job. Nicole has been working all week on the senior float."

"Maybe she won't have much time to shop for a dress," Brooke said hopefully. "Maybe if we can find me a sensational dress and I look simply gorgeous, everybody will vote for me. It is a popularity thing after all."

"I don't know," I said hesitantly, thinking that Nicole was pretty popular.

"I've taken $100 out of my savings account," Brooke whispered to me after a long pause. "Don't tell my parents, they'd kill me."

"But it's *your* savings account," I said, "and you have to have a dress for Homecoming."

"Yes, but they want that money put aside for college," she said. "I'm supposed to be saving for my share of the cost of Harvard. It's twenty thousand a year now, you know."

"Just think, if you went to San Jose State, you could splurge all that money on lots of fun things," I said, trying to cheer her up.

She looked at me in horror. "That's not even funny. If I have to go to San Jose State, I'll die."

"Hey, hold on a minute," I said. "Plenty of people are happy to go to a state school. I might end up going there if I don't get into a University of California college."

She stared ahead of her, pretending to concentrate hard on her driving. "Yes, but I always want so much," she said softly. "I want the best, Joanie. If I can't have the best, I don't want anything at all."

"Brooke, I don't think you should get your hopes up too high," I said cautiously. "There are plenty of good schools in the country where you can get a great education. It's not the end of the world if you don't get into Harvard."

"It would be the end of the world," she said flatly. "My parents would think I had let them down."

"That's baloney! They probably don't realize how many excellent students get turned down," I said. "You should set them straight right away."

"They're not very rational where I'm concerned," she said. "Oh, look. There's a parking space right outside Nordstrom's. That's a good omen, isn't it?"

Brooke did a quick tour of Nordstrom's at top speed, tried on three dresses, and declared them all totally disgusting. We then went the whole length of the mall and did a similar tour of Macy's.

"What's the matter with these stores?" she demanded, tired and bad tempered by now. "Everything they've got makes me look like a wedding cake or the curtains in a movie theater! I just want a plain, sexy dress. Is that too much to ask for?"

"We could go to Rags to Riches," I said. "They sometimes have nice stuff. Gina Parducci from school works there now."

"Gina? Do I know her?"

"Sure you do. Dark and mysterious looking. Lots of black hair—sort of a female version of Damien, I think."

"Gee, thanks a lot," Gina broke in. Joanie looked up and gave her an embarrassed smile.

Anyway, Brooke looked sort of surprised and uncomfortable when I brought up Damien's name.

"Speaking of Damien," I said, "is he going to mind your going to the dance with another guy?"

Brooke looked away. "Maybe I won't tell him,"

she said. "He's the jealous type. Anyway, I'm not going to give up a chance to be Queen just because Damien's not here. Let's go see if they've got my dress at Rags to Riches."

"I need the most wonderful dress in the world," Brooke babbled excitedly to Gina when we reached the store. "I'm a Homecoming princess, you see. And if I find the perfect dress, I might just be chosen Queen."

Gina caught my eye for a second with an expression that let me know how stupid she thought Homecoming elections were. But she probably also wanted to get the commission on selling a dress. "We've just had a new shipment in," she said. "There's some gorgeous dresses on that rack back there. Take a look at the black sequined one."

Brooke made a beeline for the rack and started working her way through it. I was secretly admiring the black sequined dress. I thought about splurging and buying it for myself. Not that I had anyone to go to the Homecoming dance with, but I was determined to go this year, even if it meant hijacking the first nerd I saw slinking down the halls. But in a flash, Brooke already had the black dress and three others over one arm.

"I'll go try these on," she said, smiling excitedly at me. "I'll call you when I'm ready for you to come and look."

The first dress was very short and white and off the shoulder. We agreed it didn't do anything for her.

"You need a long dress, so that you can sweep up to the podium to get your crown," I said.

"You're right," she said. "The other two dresses are long. I'll try them."

She disappeared again. I wandered up and down the racks and suddenly found myself staring at a shimmery blue dress. With trembling fingers I lifted it from the rack. It was delicate and simple with a tiny waist and spaghetti straps. The fabric was so lovely it almost took my breath away. It was like spun blue glass that caught the light and sparkled and glowed. I hardly dared look at the price tag: It was $130, and I knew I'd never spend that amount on a Homecoming dress.

"But you could wear it to the Christmas formal and to Senior Ball," a little voice of temptation whispered inside my head. I glanced at the tag again. It was size eight, my size!

I let myself drift into a daydream in which I floated into the dance in my blue dress. Everyone in the auditorium looked at me, noticing for the first time how pretty I was. Suddenly guys were falling over each other, trying to get to me. I was offered twenty chairs and twenty glasses of punch. A long line of guys who wanted to dance with me formed right out the door and across the parking lot.

I was just about to go ask Gina to unlock the other fitting room when Brooke emerged, wearing the black dress. "Is this sexy or what?" she asked, posing with one hand on her hip. The dress had one long sleeve and left the other shoulder and arm bare. It was slit up one side above the knee, and it sparkled with millions of sequins. It fit her like a glove.

"Wow!" I said. "You look . . ." but I never finished the sentence. Brooke had seen what I was holding in my arms.

"Where did you find that?" she asked, her voice shaky. "It is just gorgeous! How wonderful of you to find it for me!"

"Hey, wait a minute," I said. "I was just about to try it on myself."

Her face flushed bright pink. "You were about to try it on? For yourself?"

"Why not?" I asked. "I'm not Cinderella, you know. I am allowed to go to the ball, even though I'm not a princess."

"Oh sure, of course you are," she said breathlessly, "but Joanie, it's not as important what you wear."

"Gee, thanks a lot," I said.

"I didn't mean it like that," she said hurriedly. "I

mean that everyone's going to be looking at me. I have to make a good impression. It's life and death what I wear."

"Not exactly life and death," I said. "It's only Homecoming."

"Only Homecoming?" she demanded. "Anyway, I think the matter is settled, because that dress looks tiny. What size is it?"

"Size eight."

"There you go," she said with relief in her voice. "It's too small for you. See, I knew it was destined for me."

"I happen to wear a size eight now," I said.

She looked me up and down. "You? A size eight? I don't believe it. You always wear a twelve."

"I lost fifteen pounds this summer, Brooke, and I am a perfect size eight."

"But you can't be," she said, her eyes wide with amazement. "You can't be the same size as me."

"Believe it," I said. "I'll go try on the dress and then you'll see."

She put out a hand to stop me. "Joanie, please. If you're truly my best friend, if our friendship means anything to you at all, please, please let me try on the dress. The moment I saw it I knew it was right for a princess. It's just what Cinderella's fairy godmother would create for her. This is so important to me, Joanie."

47

I had had a lifetime of giving in to Brooke. Part of me wanted to be stubborn and tell her that she had gotten her own way long enough, but those blue eyes still had a great influence over me. I found myself handing the dress to her—my magic dress, the most beautiful dress I ever saw. She gave a little squeal of happiness and dove into the changing room.

When she came out a few minutes later, I had to admit that the dress looked better on her than it ever would have on me. The dress matched her eyes and set off her blond hair, which curled over her nicely tanned shoulders. She looked once more like the fairy princess she had been back in kindergarten.

"It's just right, isn't it?" she asked. "Would you really mind if I bought it?"

My head shook by itself. I heard myself saying, "Go ahead. I probably won't go. I don't even have a date."

"Oh, you have to come, Joanie," she said. I waited for her to say that the dance wouldn't be any fun without me there, but instead she went on: "You have to watch me float up to the platform to get that crown!"

All the old resentments bubbled back to the surface. So my best friend only wanted me at a dance to watch her! That was my role in life after all, watching Brooke get the dates and the awards and the glory.

"Enough is enough," I muttered to myself as I waited for Brooke to pay for the exquisite dress, which Gina carefully wrapped in oodles of pink tissue. "Enough is enough!"

Chapter Five

You know how crazy Homecoming week was. Even in my grouchy mood, I couldn't help getting caught up in the spirit of fun.

Brooke and I wore huge piles of fake fruit on our heads on Crazy Hat Day. We wore poodle skirts, bobbysox, and our hair in ponytails on Fifties Day. For Nerd Day we had a great time at the Salvation Army buying horrible skirts and cardigans in clashing colors and extra-thick glasses. On Senior Toga Day, I froze walking around in just a bed sheet, like everyone else.

Throughout those theme days I kept hoping that some sort of chance would come for me to stand out. But I didn't win the crazy hat contest on day one, and I didn't have a partner for the rock'n roll contest on day two. The tug-of-war contest took place Wednesday on the specially created mud patch beside the football field. I decided I did not want my one claim to fame to be that I was found trampled to death at the bottom of a mud puddle.

I became desperate as I tried to think of ways to be noticed: I'd take a crash course in salsa dancing and leave all the guys at the dance spellbound. This was not a very practical daydream, since when I'd taken ballet lessons at the age of six they'd made me the tree in the woodland ballet because I couldn't keep in time with all the other woodland fairies.

The week went on and I began to feel depressed. No outstanding ideas came to me, and I still didn't even have a date.

Brooke annoyed me more and more, throwing fuel on the fire of my anger and keeping it going. Not that she was being mean to me or anything. She had been extra sweet since she got the blue dress and kept saying things like, "I don't know how I'm ever going to repay you, Joanie." But it was that sweetness that was so terrible. In my frame of mind, I could only see it as a sneaky way to get exactly what she wanted from spineless, naive people like me!

On top of it, Brooke talked nonstop about the

dance, being a princess, hoping to be Queen, and Kyle Carpenter. Kyle was naturally a prince.

"Wouldn't it be perfect, Joanie," Brooke sighed, as we walked home together that Thursday afternoon, "if I was Queen and Kyle was King? Can't you just see us dancing together?"

"What about Damien?" I asked. Until then, all I had heard every time the subject of boyfriends came up was: Damien was so smart, Damien was so creative, Damien was so handsome.

"He's so far away," she said quickly. "And I won't tell him because he'd be incredibly jealous. But Kyle is right here!" She grabbed my arm and pulled me close to her. "Joanie, I never really confessed this to anyone before, but I've always had a crush on Kyle. There have been a few times when he's seemed interested in me and I thought he was going to ask me out, but then something always got in the way. This would make it so natural. . . . I'd sit beside him on the platform, they'd put crowns on our heads, and then we'd walk together down the steps, hand in hand, and dance the first dance together. He'd hold me tight and I'd put my head on his shoulder . . ."

"Watch out for the crown," I said.

"What?"

"Watch out for the crown, those spikes are sharp. You don't want to stab Kyle's shoulder, do you?"

"Oh no, of course not," she said, giggling. "Okay, so I don't put my head on his shoulder, but he still holds me tight and at the end of the dance he doesn't let go. He whispers in my ear, 'I've known you all this time, Brooke, and I never realized how perfect we are for each other.' How does that sound?"

"Wonderful," I said. I had closed my eyes for a moment and imagined that Kyle was saying those things to me. Of course, I was not even a princess so I had no chance of dancing with him.

"Now we have to do something about you," Brooke said.

"Me?"

"Yes, about finding you a date. You have to come, Joanie. It's senior year. Your last chance to come to a Homecoming dance, and I want you to be there when I win."

"I'm sure I can find myself a guy if I really try," I said.

"I'll see if I can help," Brooke said generously.

"You really don't need to."

"Oh, but I really want to, Joanie," Brooke insisted. "Let me do some calling around tonight."

Later that evening I went over to her house to help her try out hairstyles to go with the dress. Brooke's mom came in to watch.

"It was so nice of you to lend Brooke the dress, Joanie," she said. "She is so thrilled with it."

"Yes, Joanie," Brooke rushed in. "I told my mom how you bought this in a boutique in Beverly Hills last summer and were sweet enough to lend it to me because I was a princess," she said, her eyes saying clearly, "This is the story so don't blow it!"

After her mom had left the room, Brooke let out a sigh of relief.

"Phew, that was a close one."

"Why did you have to make up a dumb lie like that?" I asked.

"I'm sorry. I had no choice," she said. "I was about to show them the dress when they gave me this long lecture about finances and how their investments had not done as well as they had hoped. They said they were relying on me to save every penny I could to help out with college. I could hardly tell them I bought the dress at the Salvation Army, could I?"

"You could have checked with me first," I said.

"I didn't think you'd mind," she said, surprised.

But I do mind, Brooke Stevenson, I thought to myself as I walked home. *I have had it up to here with being used and patronized and taken for granted.*

The last day of Homecoming week dawned clear and bright, with just a nip of fall in the air. The sky was a clear arc of blue glass above us. The maples all along our street were flaming red, the oak trees in the park were dazzling yellow in the sunlight. Everything seemed to be a good omen for the day. I walked to school with quick, confident strides, not knowing why I felt so hopeful.

Brooke met me by our lockers. "Guess what?" she yelled, her voice echoing all the way down the hall. "I found you a date for the dance."

Half the school stopped walking past to hear who the lucky guy was.

"You know Carlo in the band?"

Carlo. He wasn't half bad! Tall, nice smile . . .

"He has this friend who wants to go to the dance but doesn't have a date yet. His name's Ron. He plays the tuba."

"Ron? The little fat guy with the big lips?"

"He's not that little, Joanie," Brooke said, hurt that I wasn't throwing myself to the ground in ecstasy. "And his lips are not that big."

"His lips have been caught in elevator doors!" I said. "I'd rather not come at all than be stuck with a geek for the evening. Thanks anyway."

I didn't say anything more to Brooke, but inside I felt furious. I was like a volcano, waiting to explode.

The student body assembled at lunchtime in the amphitheater. The band played. The princes and princesses were presented. Brooke and I had decided the night before what she should wear to school. She looked great in her white miniskirt and a soft blue denim shirt. But the other princesses looked great, too, especially Nicole, who was wearing hot pink shorts that showed off her tanned legs.

After the football team was introduced, the cheerleaders led cheers, and the crazy relays were held, something amazing happened.

"And now, ladies and gentlemen," Danny Russo boomed, "the moment you have all been waiting for. The famous Homecoming slave-for-a-day raffle. You've all bought your tickets, I hope? Would the princes and princesses, your future slaves, kindly step up onto the stage. Check your tickets, ladies and gentlemen, while I call out the winning numbers. Who is going to be the lucky winner of a slave for a day?"

There was much excitement in the crowd as we all found our tickets. One by one the Homecoming court was claimed by winning ticket holders. At last it was Kyle's turn. He clowned around at the edge of the stage, showing his muscles.

"This fine, healthy young man will do anything you command him to," Danny said, pinching Kyle's biceps. "He is strong and very willing!"

All the girls squealed.

"And the lucky number is . . . 34702."

"Go on, you got it," a girl behind me yelled, and

I found myself being pushed forward through the crowd.

"Way to go, Joanie," someone shouted.

I stumbled up the steps, my cheeks burning. Kyle was looking at me with amusement.

Danny, for once, looked serious.

"Madam," he said with a bow, "I have great pleasure in presenting you with your slave."

Then he reached out and put Kyle's hand in mine.

Chapter
Six

I don't know how long I stood there like a statue, my face red, my heart pounding, and Kyle's hand in mine. I was still in a dream as we were guided back down the steps.

"Okay, Joanie, so what are you going to command me to do?" he asked, grinning like a little kid. "I'm all yours for the day, so make the most of me!"

My brain had completely shut down. I stared at him like an idiot.

"Only you better hurry up," he said, "because the football team has to be down at the field by 2:00 for pregame warm-ups."

"I can't think right now," I said, "but I'll come up with something."

"Don't let him off too easily." "Yeah, make him work," voices around me were advising.

My brain was still a blank.

But as I stood there a crazy thought began to form in my mind. It was so wild, so completely outrageous that I hardly dared think it. Would I ever do something like that? If only I had the nerve . . .

"Hey, slavemasters!" came Danny's big voice, interrupting my daydream. "Are you going to give us orders or what? Your humble slaves are just standing here, waiting to see what you want us to do, and we have to go suit up for football pretty soon."

One by one the group drifted apart until it was just me and Kyle. Kyle was sitting on the edge of the platform, swinging his feet, relaxed and good-humored as always.

"So what's it going to be?" he asked. "Have you decided?"

"I think so," I said.

"Just don't dress me up like a baby, okay? I'd hate that."

"Nothing like that," I said. I was amazingly calm. I was going to be able to go through with it!

"Okay, tell me the bad news. I have to go soon," Kyle said.

"It's okay, there's no hurry," I said. "I don't need this done until after the football game."

He looked up, surprised.

"I command you to take me to the Homecoming dance," I said, and my voice didn't even wobble.

To say he was surprised would be a huge understatement. Kyle, who had never been lost for something to say, looked at me with his jaw gaping open. "You what?" he asked.

"The Homecoming dance," I said. "I want you to be my date."

"But Joanie," he began, "I'm a prince. I have to escort a princess."

"That's fine. You can escort her onto the stage when you have to, but for the rest of the dance, you're with me."

"Hey, wait a minute," he said, standing up. "This thing is only meant to be fun—a school prank."

"I was told you were my slave for the day," I said, "and the day does not end until midnight tonight."

His eyes met mine for the first time. I had never noticed what deep, clear brown eyes he had. At last he shrugged, good-naturedly. "I guess so then," he said. "You want me to pick you up at 8:30?"

"Fine," I said.

"See you then," he said. He waved easily and moved away. Only as he disappeared out of the amphitheater did my knees start shaking.

I could not believe what I had done. I felt as if I had just crossed the North Pole or swum the Pacific Ocean. I wanted to get up on the stage and yell out, "Hey, everybody, guess what! Kyle Carpenter is taking me to the dance!"

I couldn't wait to see Brooke's face when I told her. This was the only time in our entire lives together that I had gone one better than her. All those years of Brooke being Mother Nature in the first-grade play and me being a frog, of Brooke winning the art contest in third grade and me getting honorable mention, of Brooke singing the solos in chorus, attracting the boys on the beach, and being elected officer of every club and society in creation, while I got to help decorate and serve food and, most often, clean up afterward. And now, finally, I was going to stand out!

I squirmed in my seat like a kindergartner all through government class that afternoon. I spent the whole of trigonometry gazing out the window, watching the pine trees moving gracefully in the wind and imagining me and Kyle, Kyle and me, dancing together, his arms around me . . .

"Are you with us, Joanie Hammond?" Mrs. Alietti, the math teacher, demanded. "Or did you decide to take an afternoon nap so that you won't be too tired tonight?"

Everyone laughed. For once it didn't faze me one

62

bit. *Let them laugh,* I thought. *What do I care? I'm going to Homecoming with Kyle Carpenter.*

The last bell rang and everyone fought to get to the parade and football game. I hurriedly grabbed my homework assignments from my locker and tried to find Brooke. As I reached the parking lot, the band was already moving off with the class floats behind it. The noise was deafening.

I ran past it to the first float, which carried the royal court. The princesses were sitting on purple velvet steps, each wearing her formal dress and her crown. I had to admit that my blue dress looked fantastic on Brooke.

"Hey, Brooke!" I yelled up to her.

She gave a gesture to show that she couldn't hear a thing I was saying over all the noise.

"See you, Joanie," she called sweetly, and turned to wave to her loyal subjects.

The big truck revved and drove off, turning out of the parking lot. Brooke grinned and waved to me. I turned and made my way down to the football field. I was halfway down the road among the excited crowd of kids, when I suddenly realized: If I was going to the dance with Kyle, I needed a really stunning, sensational dress! I made an instant decision, wheeled out of the stream of kids, and crossed the street. Finding the right dress was far more important than cheering a dumb football team, even if Kyle was playing.

All the way to the mall I felt drunk with freedom and excitement. Tonight I was going to be with Kyle. What more in the world could anyone want?

I headed straight for Rags to Riches. I think I was secretly hoping that they'd have another dress like Brooke's—maybe not identical, but a shimmery, silky, magical creation that would make me look like a princess, too. A large lady in black was working in the store instead of Gina. I realized Gina was at the football game because her boyfriend, Andy, was one of the stars of the team.

After searching every rack for a dress like the blue one, I gave up, picked up the sexy black sequined dress, and headed for the changing room. The result was surprising. The dress fit like a second skin. I still weighed a few pounds more than Brooke, and I filled the dress out more than she did. Experimentally I pulled my hair back from my face and gave the mirror a movie-star pout. A sexy stranger looked back at me.

"I'll take it," I told the saleswoman and sailed out of the store. Having already done two crazy things in one day, there was no stopping me now. I went to a department store and bought black high-heeled shoes; matching rhinestone necklace, earrings, and bracelet; and red lipstick and nail polish.

I didn't add up the amount I was spending. I wanted everything to be perfect, whatever it cost.

The moment I got home, I rushed to my room and tried it all on—the dress and the jewels, even the red lipstick. Then I slunk out of my bedroom and stood behind my mother. "So how do I look?" I asked in my new, sexy voice.

My mother blinked a couple of times. "You're going to wear that to the dance?"

"No Mom, I'm going on a ski trip," I said. "Of course I'm wearing it to the dance. Isn't it fantastic?"

"It's a beautiful dress," she said carefully, "it's just that . . . I've never seen, I mean, you look so grown up."

"It's the new me," I said, "so you better get used to it. No more Miss Wishy-washy. No more Brooke's shadow."

"Honey, are you okay?" she asked.

"I feel wonderful," I said. "Do you realize this is the best day of my life? In just over two hours, I'll be going to the Homecoming dance with Kyle Carpenter. How about that?"

Now she really looked surprised. "Kyle Carpenter? *The* Kyle Carpenter?"

"No, a four-foot nerd who happens to have the same name," I said, grinning at her. "Of course *the* Kyle Carpenter."

"And he asked you to the dance?"

"Mom, I'm not that horrible, you know."

"Of course you're not, honey," she said hastily. "It's just that . . . I've heard about Kyle for years. He's one of the most popular boys in the school, isn't he? I was just surprised that he'd . . . um . . . wait till the last moment to ask a date." Obviously, that wasn't exactly what was surprising her.

I went back up the stairs and called Brooke from the extension in my parents' bedroom. I didn't want my mother to know the real reason I was going with Kyle. I wanted her to think that someone cute and popular liked me for myself.

Brooke's mother answered the phone. "Oh, hello, Joanie. Yes, she just got home, but I made her go and rest. She's been looking so tired lately, have you noticed? I think she's doing too much. I wish I could get her to drop volleyball and concentrate on her studies."

"But she loves volleyball," I said.

Brooke's mother sighed. "She's so gifted, and she has such wonderful opportunities opening up for her if she can just keep her mind on her goals and work hard all year."

She paused as if I ought to say something so I made a sort of coughing sound. She went on, "It's so important that she keep up her grades this year. Harvard isn't going to care if she plays volleyball or not. I'd rather she spent more time on the important things, like the French club and the debating society. Maybe you can talk to her about it, Joanie."

"I have to go get ready now," I said. "Would you ask her to call me when she wakes up?"

Parents! I thought as I hung up. *Brooke's expect her to be perfect and mine think I'm a hopeless case!*

Chapter
Seven

I was naturally in the shower when Brooke called me. If you ever want an important phone call, all you have to do is go into the shower and the phone will ring right away. I came out dripping wet with the towel around me.

"Hi," she said. "What's up? I can't talk long. I have to get showered and dressed for tonight."

"I just got in the shower, too," I said, "but I had to tell you!"

"You're coming to the dance tonight?" she asked.

"I sure am."

"That's great, Joanie," she said. "Did you find someone nice to take you?"

"Yeah," I said, grinning, "I'm going with Kyle."

"I'm sorry," she said. "I thought for a moment you said you were going with Kyle."

"That's right. You heard correctly," I said. "Joanie Hammond is going to the dance with Kyle Carpenter!"

"Dream on!" Brooke said.

"You don't believe me?"

"You can't be serious."

"Wait until 8:30 tonight and you'll see how serious I am."

I heard Brooke's sputtered laughter on the other end of the line. "You're trying to tell me that Kyle asked you to the dance?"

"Why not?" I said, suddenly not wanting her to know the truth. The giggle on the other end of the phone hurt and annoyed me.

"It's probably some sort of joke," she said. "You know Kyle."

"Thanks a lot," I said. "I thought you were supposed to be my best friend. You think I'd only be asked as some sort of joke?"

"I'm sorry, Joanie," she said, "but I'm just trying to be realistic. I know you're a very nice person but you're not . . . well, you know . . . Anyway, Kyle is a prince. He's supposed to escort one of the princesses."

"I talked to Kyle about that," I said. "I told him I understood that he'd have to dance with a princess, and if he's chosen King, he'll have to dance with the Queen, but the rest of the time, he's with me."

"I just don't get this, Joanie," Brooke said, her voice no longer sounding amused. "When did all this happen? How come I didn't hear about it?"

"It only came up this afternoon," I said.

"I still don't believe it," she snapped.

"Come on, Brooke," I said. "This is the most exciting thing that's ever happened to me. For once I get to be in the spotlight. I thought you might be happy for me!"

"Happy for you?" she demanded, her voice high and tight now. "Why should I be happy for you? I thought that you were my best friend, Joanie. You knew I was hoping to spend the evening with Kyle. I imagined that if I got elected Queen and he got to be King . . . Did you do this deliberately to spite me?"

"Of course not," I said. It was my turn to be surprised. I knew she thought Kyle was gorgeous. We all did. We'd all had an ongoing crush on him since freshman year. I knew she had fantasized about dancing with Kyle, but so had I. It had never occurred to me that she intended to go after him

71

seriously. "I had no idea you really wanted Kyle," I said. "I thought you still liked Damien."

"Damien? If I could have Kyle? Are you serious?" she demanded. "You must have known why I wanted to look good tonight!"

"I thought it was to go on your Harvard application," I said. "Look, Brooke, I had no idea I was spoiling your chances. How many times have you told me that you didn't want to get involved with a boy this year because you didn't have time for it?"

"That statement did not include Kyle," she said. "It would be like turning down the winning lottery ticket because you had said you were happy with the amount of money you already had. I would die for the chance to have Kyle for a boyfriend. You should have known that."

"And you should have known I've worshipped him since I first saw him, too. I'm not giving up my one chance, even for you. All's fair in love and war."

"You don't seriously think you've got a chance with him?" she asked, a sharp edge to her voice now.

"I never thought this day would come," I said, enjoying the feeling of power. "I believe that Brooke Stevenson is jealous of Joanie Hammond for the first time in her life!"

"Jealous of you?" Brooke asked. She gave a fake, high laugh. "That's really funny, Joanie. Why would I ever be jealous of you?"

"Because we both like the same guy and it looks as if I've got him."

"Come on, Joanie," Brooke said. "If I decide to go after Kyle, if I show him that I'm really interested, do you think he'd look at you twice?"

"I don't know," I said. "We'll just have to see tonight, won't we?"

Then I hung up. I think it was the first time in my life that I had put the phone down first. I felt excited and scared at the same time. Brooke and I hardly ever fought. *But that was because I usually gave in,* I decided. Now I was being assertive for the first time, and Brooke did not like it. *She better get used to it,* I told myself, *because I don't intend to be her shadow any longer!*

For a moment I had totally forgotten the circumstances that had gotten me the date with Kyle. I was so riled up after fighting with Brooke that I think I seriously believed he had asked me to the dance and forgotten that I had forced him to take me.

I took a long time dressing and fixing my hair. I wanted everything to look perfect, but my hair just would not stay where I wanted it. I tried sweeping it back, but wisps kept escaping. In frustration I piled on more and more gel until I looked as if I were wearing a plastic wig. Then I had to wash it all off and start again, only this time I wasn't so ambitious. I just took one side back and held it in a comb, then I curled the other side around my face. Then I put on the red fingernail polish and the red lipstick. "Not bad at all," I said to my mirror image. At least people would think I looked different!

Kyle certainly did when I opened my front door at 8:30.

"Is Joanie . . ." he began, then I saw his eyes open wider. "Joanie? Wow! Nice dress," he said. "You look great."

"Thank you," I said joyfully.

"You ready?" he asked. "We'd better step on it. I've got Paul and his date in the car, and I told the guys we'd meet them outside the gym at 8:45."

So much for my fantasy of arriving alone with Kyle. Instead of sitting beside him in the front seat, I was squished into the back with Darlene Sanders. Darlene had one of those dresses with about fifty layers of net in the skirt that took up most of the seat. "Watch out for my dress," she said as I tried to sit down. I lowered myself onto the last three inches of the seat and held my breath all the way to school.

There was a crowd of kids outside the auditorium as we pulled up. At least I got the satisfaction of Kyle offering me his hand to help me out of the fetal position I had been riding in. I straightened up painfully in time to see Danny and a couple of other guys coming toward us. Danny's face broke into a big grin when he saw Kyle, but the grin faded as he saw me beside him.

"Hey, buddy? What's happening?" he called to Kyle. His eyes clearly indicated, *What on earth is she doing with you?*

"Why don't you go on in, Joanie," Kyle said. "Danny and I have to talk strategy about this prince stuff. I'll catch up with you."

I walked on ahead but not fast enough. Danny's voice was not made for secrecy. Even his whisper echoed off the concrete steps.

"You're kidding, man! She can't make her slave do stuff like that. It's supposed to be fun. Why didn't you tell her?"

I didn't hear Kyle's reply. Music was spilling loudly out of the open auditorium doors. Even the ground was vibrating to the beat. I went through the big double doors and was stopped by the crowd in the hallway, waiting to buy tickets to get into the dance. I could see the flash of colored lights inside the auditorium and swaying silhouettes of people dancing. The crowd closed in around me, and I was swallowed up. Then I heard Kyle's voice right behind me.

"Don't worry about it," he was saying to Danny.

"I told her I'd take her, all right? All I have to do is walk in through that door with her. After that, she's on her own! Get Nicole to save me a place at your table. I'll dance with her a couple of times, give her a little hug in the slow number, then say I have to go to the men's room and disappear. Should only take a few minutes."

My cheeks were flaming, and the crowd was suddenly oppressive, squeezing the life out of me. I couldn't breathe. I had to get out of there or I would have fainted. I fought blindly, pushing people out of the way to get through those big double doors. On my way out, stumbling blindly, I pushed past Kyle.

"Hey, Joanie, where you going?" he asked. "Did you forget something?"

"Yes," I said. "I forgot that I was me! It's okay, I'll save you the trouble of ditching me. I'll go call my dad to come get me right now."

I pushed past him and stepped out of the crowded hallway into the crisp night air. I started walking across the parking lot, my high heels tapping lightly on the asphalt. I don't know where I thought I was going. There was no public phone between school and my house. I just wanted to walk fast, to put distance between me and my embarrassment. I had almost reached the front gate when Kyle caught up with me.

"Joanie, wait up," he said, breathlessly, as if he'd been sprinting. "Wait a minute."

"Why?" I asked. "So that everybody can watch you ditch me and get a good laugh out of it?" I looked away from him, studying the curly wrought iron of the gates. "It's okay. I release you from being my slave. You can go back to your friends. I should have realized this was too good to be true. Things like this don't happen in real life, do they?"

I felt him hesitate beside me. "Does it really mean so much to you to go this dance with me?" he asked quietly.

I was biting my lip now, afraid that I'd disgrace myself and cry. "I just wanted . . . once in my life . . ." I mumbled.

"Wanted what?"

"To go to one high school dance," I said. "To do the things Brooke gets to do."

He looked at me in astonishment. "You've never been to a dance?" he asked.

I shook my head. "Not a formal one. I went to the freshman welcome dance. You didn't need a date."

"Wow," he said.

"That's why I couldn't believe my luck today," I said. "I had a slave who had to do what I told him to. I'm sorry. It was dumb of me. I guess I didn't think it would embarrass you."

"Why would it embarrass me?" he asked.

"To be stuck at a dance with me," I said. "Everyone would have guessed right away that you weren't doing it by choice. I realize that now."

He was still looking at me, as if he realized for the first time that I was a person and not a shadow that tagged behind Brooke. "Look, Joanie," he said, running his tongue over his bottom lip nervously, "if it really means so much to you, then I'd be happy to be your date."

"You really don't have to," I said.

"You're right," he said. "I don't have to. You know me. I've never been known to do anything I didn't want to. Did I ever show up once when we were doing folk dancing in P.E.? I can always think up excuses when I don't want to do something—I strained my big toe, it's a religious holiday, the dog ate my sneaker . . ."

He started laughing and so did I.

"So you see," he said, "if I say I'd be happy to be your date, I really mean it. I'll have to do my stuff with the princesses, but apart from that, it's just you and me, babe. What do you say?"

I couldn't find the words. I just stood there, nodding silently. Over the years I'd always heard what a nice guy Kyle was. I'd just found out how nice.

"Come on," he said, grabbing my hand, "they're

playing a song I really like. Let's get back in there before it's over."

I don't think my feet touched the asphalt once between the gate and the steps.

Chapter
Eight

The dance was just as I had imagined it in my wildest fantasies. Kyle and I danced nonstop. He leapt around crazily to the fast songs and held me tightly during the slow ones. I could see people looking at us, many of the girls with envy. Several people told me I looked great in my dress. One girl said, "I hadn't heard about you and Kyle," which made me feel like a million dollars.

The most amazing thing of all was that it wasn't just wonderful being with a guy who seemed to me like a god. I was truly having a great time. Kyle was so much fun to be with.

"Okay, Joanie, let's dance the Gorilla!" he'd say

and start jumping around like a gorilla, or "Let's do the jitterbug!" It didn't seem to matter that we were doing weird things. Other people usually started copying Kyle, and pretty soon the whole dance floor was full of gorillas, or couples jitterbugging, or whatever the music suggested to Kyle. On the slow songs we pointed out things that made us laugh.

"Why is it that puny guys always dance with big girls?" he whispered in my ear. "Look at that couple over there."

I saw a large girl draped all over a guy who must have been a foot shorter than she was.

"He looks like he's being swallowed by an octopus," I whispered back, and Kyle laughed loudly.

"Those two in the middle," I whispered. "I bet they learned to dance by numbers: One, put your left foot forward, two, put your right forward . . ." We watched as they proceeded down the floor with grim determination, then we looked at each other and laughed again.

It became a game to make secret comments about other couples and then try to keep a straight face as we danced close to them. I was having such a great time that I almost forgot about the crowning of the King and Queen. But at 10:30 there was a drumroll and Kyle let go of my hand.

"Gotta go do my royal stuff now," he said. "See ya later."

The princes and princesses assembled on stage, the princes looking incredibly handsome in their tuxes and the princesses frothing with yards of shimmering skirts in various pastels, except for Nicole. She was in that plain white sheath with long sleeves and a low neck, which looked dramatic against her tan. Mrs. Oliver stepped up to the microphone. "The votes have been counted," she said. "The envelope please."

As you probably remember, everyone laughed as Mr. Peters brought out a silver tray with an envelope on it—everyone except Brooke, that is. I could tell she was forcing herself to smile, and her eyes darted from the principal to the other contestants and back again.

"It gives me great pleasure to present to you your King and Queen," Mrs. Oliver said, looking up from the envelope, "Kyle Carpenter and Nicole Summers."

The crowd went wild. I was yelling and clapping too, thrilled as if I was in some way responsible for Kyle's success. He looked so incredible, standing up there waving, then clowning around in his Richard Nixon impersonation, as Mrs. Oliver put a crown on his head. Nicole didn't look surprised that she had won; she stood there smiling, composed and elegant beside him. I had to admit, they made a great pair as they posed for pictures. Then Kyle led

Nicole down the steps and began a slow dance with her while we all applauded.

Brooke still had the fixed smile on her face, but it looked as if it might crack at any moment. *She really wanted to win this badly,* I thought, watching her. *She's always telling me to be realistic about things, but she wasn't realistic about her chances of winning. I could have told her Nicole would win.*

Kyle and Nicole turned together slowly on the floor. In the past I would have watched enviously, wishing it could be me, but tonight it didn't worry me that Nicole was in Kyle's arms. He had held me like that, he had looked down at me and smiled like that. I was totally and completely content.

As I stood there in the darkness at the edge of the crowd, Brooke pushed past me.

"Hi," I said. "I'm sorry you didn't win. The dress looks great."

Her eyes narrowed as she looked at me. "I told you in the store that we weren't the same size. You should have taken me shopping with you. That dress is way too small for you. It's indecent, Joanie."

"Kyle seems to like it." I said.

"Oh sure," Brooke said. "You really had me fooled for a minute there."

"What do you mean?" I asked.

Her face was very flushed. "I mean I almost believed that Kyle had asked you tonight."

"You saw us dancing."

"Sure," Brooke said, "and I know why he was dancing with you, too. You should have told me the truth in the first place, Joanie. You knew I'd find out anyway."

"Meaning what?"

"That you tricked him into taking you to the dance with that stupid slave-for-a-day contest. I danced with Paul and he told me. I'm sure everyone else knows by now, too. I bet they were all giggling behind your back while you danced with him."

I looked at her as if I were seeing her for the first time. "You don't like me very much, do you?" I asked. "I really thought you were my best friend. All these years I thought we were best friends, and now I realize that we never were. Talk about me making use of a slave for a day! You've had a slave for thirteen years. Now that I've stopped obeying your every command, you can't handle it, can you?"

"I don't know what you're talking about," she said, her face even redder now. "It's because I'm your best friend that I'm trying to make you face reality. You know Kyle wouldn't have noticed your existence if he hadn't been stuck with you today, so don't fool yourself into thinking it's anything more than that."

"If you really were my best friend, you'd be glad I finally got a chance with Kyle," I said.

"If it had been a real chance, sure," she said, "but no guy is going to like you after you forced him to take you to a dance. I don't know what's gotten into you lately, Joanie. You used to be such a sweet person. Why are you trying to be something you're not?"

"You mean a threat to you?" I couldn't resist saying it.

I thought Brooke was going to hit me for a moment. "You?" she demanded. "How could you be a threat to me? We're not even in the same ballpark. We're not even in the same league!" She looked out across the floor where Kyle was dancing with Nicole, her arms draped around his shoulders. "Anyway, Cinderella, the party's over. Kyle's with Nicole now. I guess it's pumpkin time again!"

As she finished talking the music ended, and her last words echoed loudly through the room. Kyle kissed Nicole on the cheek and headed in my direction.

"Hey, Joanie," he called. "The King commands! Get over here! I've done my duty with Nicole. You ready to get down and boogie again?"

I turned back to Brooke and gave her my sweetest smile. "Would you excuse me?" I asked. "My presence is needed on the dance floor!" I glided across the floor to Kyle, savoring every second of it.

"What's with Brooke?" Kyle asked as took my hand and started to move to the rhythm of the music. "If looks could kill, they'd be carrying you out of here in a pine box right now. You two have a fight?"

"You could say that. She's mad at me for dancing with you. She said some horrible things."

"Like what?"

"She found out about the slave-for-a-day thing and told me I was making a fool of myself, trying to be something I'm not."

"And what are you trying to be?" Kyle asked, his eyes flashing with amusement.

"A girl who's having a good time, I guess," I said. "Apparently Brooke is allowed to have a good time, but I'm supposed to sit home knitting."

"And are you having a good time?" he asked.

"Wow," I said, shaking my head in disbelief that he could even doubt it. "I'd like to put this evening in a little box and treasure it for the rest of my life."

"Don't you think there will be bigger and better evenings than this?" he asked. "There's Senior Ball coming up, and then college—all sorts of good stuff. I don't expect this to be the highlight of my life."

"I can understand that," I said, "but then you're always going to be at the center of things. You're that kind of person. I'm not. That's why I'm really grateful that you've made me feel so special tonight. I know you could be dancing with any girl in this room right now."

"That's me, Mr. Wonderful," he said, flashing me the famous grin. "I wonder if they'll give me a medal for this?" Then he grabbed my shoulders and shook me hard. "Listen to me, you idiot! I've had a great time this evening. I've had a great time being with you. You're funny and you're quick and you dance well."

"Really?"

He continued to hold my shoulders, digging in his fingers almost until it hurt. "You've got to stop feeling sorry for yourself. There's no reason why you shouldn't have as much fun as any other girl in this room. There's nothing wrong with you and there's a lot that's right!"

The band struck up "Twist and Shout." Kyle let go of my shoulders. "Come on, let's do the Twist!" he yelled, and soon we were in a mass of twisting bodies all singing along. The feeling of being part of it, right in the middle of things, was overpowering. I felt so happy I wanted to burst. I sang as loudly as anyone. I didn't want it to end ever.

Chapter
Nine

Of course the dance did come to an end, promptly at midnight. Mrs. Oliver stepped out onto the stage, told the band to play the last song, and warned us all to drive home safely. I danced the last song with Kyle, my head on his shoulder, enjoying the feel of his jacket against my cheek and the smell of his cologne. We met Paul and Darlene outside, and I climbed into the back seat of the car beside Darlene. I felt like a balloon slowly deflating. It was all over. Tomorrow I was back to being Joanie again.

"I don't feel like going home yet," Kyle said. "Let's go get a cup of coffee somewhere. There's the coffee shop down on El Camino that's open twenty-four hours."

We drove to the coffee shop, and Kyle ordered us all cappuccinos. It was the first time I had tried one, and I loved the frothy, chocolatey taste of the milk on top. It was impossible to drink without getting a white moustache, and we all laughed at each other.

"So what are we doing tomorrow?" Kyle asked Paul. "Do you think it's going to be beach weather?"

"We ought to work on the play," Paul said, "or we'll never get it finished in time to enter."

Kyle made a face. "Oh yeah, I guess we should. Bummer."

"What play is this?" Darlene asked.

Kyle made a face. "Ask your boyfriend," he said. "It was his dumb idea."

"It's not a dumb idea," Paul said. "I merely volunteered us to write a play for the district one-act festival. Our school hasn't won in living memory, and I thought it was about time we did."

Darlene looked at me and grinned. "So you two Shakespeares are going to write the next *Hamlet?*" she asked.

"Much better than *Hamlet,*" Paul said. "We're writing a psychological thriller about a girl who's in the house alone and somebody keeps calling her. It's good stuff."

"Only we've written about five lines and the one-act festival is at the beginning of December," Kyle said. "We really need it finished and in rehearsal in the next couple of weeks, but I don't see how . . ." He stopped talking and turned to me. "You're good with words," he said. "What this play needs is some lightening up when the tension gets too great, you know, like *Hamlet*'s grave digger? I bet you'd be great."

"Me?" I asked.

"Joanie can be really funny," Kyle said to Paul. "She's got a great way of putting things. We could really use her." He turned back to me. "So how about it, Joanie?"

I blushed as three pairs of eyes looked at me. I couldn't believe I was actually being invited to help write the play.

"I'd love to," I said. "But I should warn you that I've never written a play before."

"That makes three of us," Paul said, and we all laughed.

"I've got a great idea," Kyle said. "How about we drive out to the beach tomorrow and work on the play there? That way we can keep up our tans."

"Great idea," Paul said.

"Yeah," I said. "What's Shakespeare without a tan?"

"And what about me?" Darlene asked, laughing. "Am I included in this?"

"Sure," Paul said. "You can keep us supplied with food and drink while we create."

"Gee, thanks," Darlene said. "You're too good to me."

We sat talking long after we had finished our cappuccinos, and then Kyle drove me home. It was after 1:30 when I let myself into the house and started to tiptoe to my room.

"Joanie?" a voice called from the darkened living room, and there was my mother, sitting in Dad's armchair, waiting for me.

"Oh, hi, Mom," I said. "You shouldn't have waited up."

"Do you know what time it is?" she asked. "Your father was ready to call the police."

"What do you mean?" I asked, genuinely surprised.

"The dance ended at midnight. We started to worry when you weren't home by 12:30. I called Brooke's house and she didn't know where you were."

"I just went to a coffee shop with friends," I said. "We felt like talking after the dance, that's all. There's no need for the Spanish Inquisition!"

She got up and came into the lighted hall, her hair all flattened where she had been sleeping on it.

"It's just so unlike you, Joanie," she said. "You always do things with Brooke. You've never . . ."

"Go on, say it," I said. "I've never had friends before, right?"

"I didn't mean it like that," she said. "You've always had friends."

"But not these friends," I said, "not Kyle Carpenter." Suddenly my excitement bubbled up again. I took my mother and spun her around in the middle of the floor. "Guess what, Mom? Kyle and Paul want *me* to write a play with them! We're all going to the beach tomorrow and we're going to work on the play and our tans at the same time. Doesn't that sound fantastic?"

My mother still looked puzzled. "And this isn't something Brooke's involved in?"

"No Brooke," I said firmly. "I am my own person now. I don't need her anymore."

My mother's frown deepened. "She's been a good friend to you, Joanie. Remember how shy you always were? She's done a lot of nice things for you."

"That was before I started wanting a life of my own," I said. "She doesn't seem to like the thought of me enjoying myself, too. She wants me to be the faithful servant, sitting at home and waiting for her."

"I'm sure Brooke's not like that," my mother said. "She's a lovely girl."

"Not recently," I said. "She's really changed. She keeps putting me down to make herself feel better."

"I don't understand it," my mother said.

"Neither do I," I said, "but I'm not going to let it upset me. I'm going to have a great senior year whether Brooke likes it or not. Starting with tomorrow and a day at the beach with two super-cute guys."

"I don't know, Joanie."

I went over and kissed her on her forehead. She was a lot shorter than me. I left her standing in the front hall and started up the stairs. "Thanks for waiting up for me," I said. "You didn't have to. I'm a big girl now."

I was in bed before I realized it was the first time I had handled my mother like that. I had been calm and firm and had told her how I felt. *This has to be a record for the number of firsts in twenty-four hours,* I thought with a grin as I fell asleep.

The next morning I woke to the most perfect fall day. I lay in bed, trying to remember why I was so excited. Then it came back to me: the dance and now the day at the beach with Kyle. This immediately brought up the problem of what to wear. I had two bathing suits. One was a blue-and-white Speedo, suitable for swim meets, lifeguarding, and any formal aquatic functions. The other was a very sexy black bikini that my sister had persuaded me to buy in L.A. after I had lost weight. I had worn it around the pool at her apartment complex a couple of times, but I hadn't dared wear it when anyone I knew was watching. I stared at it now, trying to decide. The Speedo was definitely boring, but I didn't want Kyle to think I was throwing myself at him by wearing the bikini. Suddenly I remembered that Brooke had the cutest Tahitian-print one-piece, high cut in the leg and low in the back. It would have been perfect. I was about to rush to the phone when I also remembered that we were in a terrible fight. Somehow it took away some of the thrill of going out with Kyle, knowing that I couldn't call Brooke and tell her about it.

Reverting to my former, sensible self, I put on the one-piece and shoved the bikini into my bag, just in case. The moment Kyle's car horn sounded outside, I forgot all thoughts of Brooke. Nothing was going to spoil this day for me, not even a fight with my best friend!

Fall in California is often the best weather of the year, but always being in school I'd hardly noticed it. From the moment Kyle picked me up it was as if all my senses had woken up at once. Kyle had the top down on his convertible, and the wind in my face gave me a wonderful feeling of freedom. We turned from suburban streets onto the highway. I had never seen the sky such a perfect deep blue before. The mountains were etched in a deeper blue against the clear sky. Here and there a poplar or oak tree flamed brilliant yellow against the evergreens and gray eucalyptus. The air was full of the scent of pine and redwood. The radio was blasting, and we drove fast. Kyle sat at the wheel, his dark curls blown by the wind, one arm resting on the door. He looked totally relaxed as he flew around one curve after another. I was both terrified and enjoying every moment of it.

I watched the trees flash past until the road crested the summit and there, before us, rivaling the sky for blueness, was the Pacific, decorated with just a few wisps of white fog a mile or so off shore.

"Look, no fog!" Kyle yelled to us. "It's going to be great!"

The road reached the ocean, and we continued southward, hugging the sides of sheer cliffs then dropping down to small deserted beaches littered with driftwood. On some of the windy parts I glanced down at the 200-foot drop to rocks and surf and closed my eyes. Kyle didn't seem to notice he wasn't driving through suburban Sunnyvale. At last we pulled off at a state beach where several boys in wet suits were already unloading surfboards from a VW Bug. Kyle and Paul took their boards from the trunk and we womenfolk carried the blankets and the cooler to a sheltered spot in the dunes.

"Look at those waves!" Kyle exclaimed. "We have to surf first."

"Man, look at the size of that one!" Paul said, grinning at Kyle.

A huge wall of water crested, broke into white foam, and rushed toward the beach carrying the arms, legs and surfboards of several surfers who had underestimated its power. Kyle started peeling off his jeans. "Come on, dude, let's get out there. I want one like that!" he yelled.

"I don't know, man, that was awful big!" Paul said, not undressing as quickly.

Kyle laughed, his whole face alight. "That's how I like 'em," he said. "Last one in is a chicken!" He grabbed his board and sprinted for the water.

"Hey, man, what about your wet suit?" Paul yelled.

"No time!" Kyle yelled as he flung his board into the first of the waves and began paddling out.

Paul stood there, torn between following his friend and putting on his wet suit. Common sense won out. He began to pull on the wet suit. "He's crazy," he said to us, not taking his eyes off Kyle once. "That water can't be more than fifty degrees."

Another big wave reared from the ocean. We saw several black, wet-suited bodies, glistening like seals, catch the wave and rise on their boards. One pale body stood effortlessly among them, moving up and down the wave, letting it tower over him then riding it back to the crest again. As he gained speed, riding it faster and faster, he let out a great whoop of joy.

"That's Kyle for you," Darlene said.

I nodded, not taking my eyes off Kyle for a second. It was like watching a superhero.

"I really don't think it's bikini weather, do you?" I heard Darlene ask behind me. "I'm keeping my T-shirt on for a while. This wind is cold."

I kept my T-shirt on, too, glad that I didn't have to make the Speedo/bikini decision. When Kyle finally came in his teeth were chattering and his skin was covered with goose bumps.

"C . . . c . . . can you p . . . p . . . pass me my towel, Joanie?" he asked. My hand touched his as I gave it to him. It felt like ice.

"You're crazy," I said. "You have a perfectly good wet suit sitting here."

"C . . . c . . . couldn't wait," he said, grinning at me. "See, the waves are not so good now." He wrapped himself in towels and lay down on the blanket like a little kid. "Rub my back, Joanie. I'm so cold," he said.

I rubbed, not quite able to get over the magic of touching him, of my hands moving up and down his back, making him warm again. Kyle closed his eyes and seemed to fall asleep.

Paul came back shortly after. "Man, it's cold in there," he said. "My toes feel like they're about to fall off. I need something to eat."

At the sound of the cooler being opened, Kyle opened his eyes and sat up. "Ah, food," he said, and grabbed a fried chicken leg. "Pass me a beer, Paul."

"Sure thing," Paul said. "Help yourselves if you want one," he added, looking at Darlene and me.

This was something I hadn't had to deal with before. As I watched the boys flicking the tabs back and putting the cans to their mouths, I wanted to say something, but I didn't want them to think I was totally uncool.

"Um . . . isn't one of you supposed to be the designated driver?" I asked, trying not to sound worried.

They both looked at me with amusement. "What?" Kyle asked.

"I just wondered which of you was going to drive home, if you both drink," I said.

Kyle's grin spread. "We only brought one six-pack with us," he said. "It takes way more than that to affect me or Paul. But if you're worried, why don't you drink one? Then I'll only have two."

"Um . . . no thanks," I said.

Darlene had a beer, and I began to wonder whether I wasn't completely uptight. Was I the only senior who didn't drink? I knew kids from school drank at parties, but I'd never gone to that kind of party. Brooke went to some of those parties. Did she drink beer? I wondered.

After lunch we played Frisbee and paddleball, and then the boys went surfing again. I was glad that I was not wearing the bikini because the boys played a very physical team-Frisbee game and expected me to dive for everything. I was glad that Darlene was worse at it than I was. We were headed home when we realized we hadn't touched the play. Paul remembered it first.

"Hey, man, we never did any work on the play."

"You're right. But we could hardly pass up good surfing weather, could we? Those might have been the last great waves of the fall. We'll just have to work on the play this week. How are your evenings, Joanie? I'll give you our ideas before school tomorrow and then maybe we can get together one evening and work on it."

"Fine with me," I said.

"Let's make it Tuesday," Kyle said. "That's the only evening I'm free."

"I have my church youth group on Tuesdays," Paul said.

"That's okay. Joanie and I can do without you," Kyle said.

"I can probably get out of it," Paul said quickly.

For the first time I began to wonder. Kyle and I

had been to the beach and not touched the play we were supposed to be working on. He wanted to get together on the one evening Paul had something else. Could it possibly be that Kyle did like me after all?

I thought about it all the way home. It helped keep my mind off the fact that I was driving with a guy who had had three beers. When we pulled up safely outside my house I had to admit that my worries had been for nothing. He did drive very well, and the beer had not seemed to affect him at all. I really did believe he was a superhero, that nothing in the world could hurt him.

Chapter
Ten

When I got to school the next morning, Brooke was waiting for me by my locker.

"You walked to school without me," she said.

"I didn't think we were still friends," I answered, not looking at her as I opened my locker and began stuffing books into it.

"It's sort of dumb to let one little fight spoil all those years of being friends, isn't it?" she asked quietly.

"I wasn't the one who said all the mean things," I answered, busy with my books.

I heard her clear her throat. "I know. I was horrible on Saturday night," she said. "I'm sorry."

"It's okay," I said, still looking away.

"I don't know what got into me," she went on. "I felt like I had to win or die. I had the world's worst evening. Nicole beat me out as Queen. I had to watch her getting crowned. Then I had to dance with stupid Raymond because he was a prince. He spent the whole evening stepping on my toes, breathing garlic down my neck and making dumb jokes. And then watching you with Kyle. I guess something just snapped."

I looked at her for the first time. "You were taking the whole thing too seriously," I said. "It was only a high school contest. In a couple of years nobody will even remember who was Queen and who wasn't."

"I know," she said. "I've switched into this got-to-win mode, and I can't seem to get out of it. I'm grabbing at anything that I can put on my applications. If I can get enough stuff, it's bound to impress them, even at places like Harvard, right?"

"It's not worth making yourself a nervous wreck, is it? Don't you want to enjoy your senior year? I know I do."

She shrugged her shoulders, helplessly. "I keep thinking that if I can just get through this year and go to a good college, I'll have my parents off my back."

I didn't know what to say to that, because it was

true. "Just tell them you're trying your hardest and you can't do any more," I said.

"You try telling them. They won't listen," she said. "Do you know what my dad said when I got home from the dance and told them I didn't win? He said, 'I hope you haven't put valuable time into this when you should have been studying for your SATs.' He didn't even say he was sorry I lost."

I nodded with understanding now. "They're being unfair. Try to ignore them," I said.

"You're so lucky that your parents don't expect much from you," she said. "You can go to San Jose State and everyone will be happy."

There it was again, the put-down to make her feel better. Just when I was trying to be supportive. It made me angry. "I might decide to apply to UCLA's film school," I said.

Her eyes opened wide. "How come?"

"I have a talent for writing plays," I said. "At least Kyle seems to think so. I'm going to be writing one with him for the one-act festival."

I couldn't have surprised her more if I'd told her I was secretly married to Tom Cruise. "You and Kyle?" she asked. "You're writing a play together? How did you force him into that one?"

"He asked me, as a matter of fact," I said. "When we went out for coffee together, after the dance. We were supposed to be working on it at the beach together yesterday, but somehow we didn't get around to it." I gave those last words lots of meaning.

"You're kidding, Joanie," she said, laughing nervously.

"Ask him if you want."

"But why you?" she blurted out.

"He likes my sense of humor," I said. "And I think he might even like me, really like me, I mean. Not just as a friend."

"Kyle likes you?"

"I'm not sure," I said. "It's too early to tell."

Brooke was shaking her head. "There has to be something behind this," she said. "Are you sure you're not making this up, Joanie?"

"Why would I make it up?" I stared at her so hard that she looked away.

"Well . . . look how you pretended that Kyle had asked you to the dance, when you had actually tricked him into taking you."

"Wrong," I said. "It was true that I made him take me, but I realized that was stupid and let him off the hook. That was when he said he wanted to take me anyway. And nobody made him invite me to the beach yesterday. I don't see why you think it's so strange that a boy finally likes me."

"It's not a boy," Brooke snapped. "It's Kyle Carpenter. He could have anyone he wants. You're a nice person, Joanie, but you're not . . . you're not *spectacular.*"

"Maybe he's tired of spectacular," I said. "Maybe he wants warm and friendly and nice for a change."

The bell for first period rang.

"Gotta go," I said. "Maybe at lunch you can judge for yourself whether I'm lying about Kyle."

Brooke's face flushed. "I'm not having lunch today," she said. "I have so much work to do, I'm spending lunch hour in the library again."

"But you have to eat," I said. "I'll sneak you something into the library if you want."

She shook her head again, more forcefully this time. "I ate way too much over the weekend," she said. "It will do me good to skip lunch."

"Come on, Brooke." I said. "You need a break."

"I also need to finish a paper for English. I have to go, Joanie. I'll meet you after school, if you aren't getting a ride home with Kyle."

I could see she almost said it as a joke.

"I don't think so today," I said. "He has football practice. Anyway, tomorrow is when we've made plans to get together."

I grabbed my books and hurried off. Out of the corner of my eye I could see her standing there, watching me go. For once I had given her something to think about. Good old predictable Joanie was beginning to do the unexpected.

After school Brooke was waiting on the steps.

"Guess what I heard," she said, falling into step beside me. "Danny is having a party on Friday night. Now we'll be able to see whether Kyle really likes you or not. If he likes you he'll invite you to Danny's party, right?"

"I guess so," I said. "Maybe he'll ask me when we're alone together tomorrow night."

The next evening I could hardly wait for Kyle to come pick me up. I must have changed outfits a dozen times in the half hour between 7:00 and 7:30. The minidress my sister Jackie had made me buy in L.A. was too sexy. My long flowery skirt was too blah. I really needed Brooke to look through my wardrobe and say, "Wear this, it's exactly right," but Brooke and I had parted coldly a couple of hours earlier.

I had decided on faded jeans and my sister's oversize UCLA sweatshirt by the time Kyle's car drove up. The jeans made me look tall and slim and couldn't give any wrong impressions.

"Hi, Joanie, ready to write a masterpiece?" he asked as he opened the car door for me.

"I hope so," I said. "I've never tried anything like this before."

"You'll be terrific."

We reached his house, big and impressive and way up in a canyon. We went up a flight of steps to the front door, which opened into a big entrance hall with a curved stairway leading upstairs. We were halfway up when a fashionably dressed, dark-haired woman came out of the living room below. She glanced up at us.

"Oh, hi, baby," she said. "You know what your father said about dates on school nights."

"This isn't a date, Mom, it's just Joanie," Kyle said. "We're working on a play together. Remember, I told you about it?"

I could see that she didn't remember. She grabbed her purse and keys from the hall table. "Tell your father I'm at the golf-club directors' meeting. He can find some cold beef in the fridge if he's hungry," she said, and swept out the door without saying a word to me.

Kyle made a funny face. "That's my mother," he said, "as you probably figured out. Off to run another committee."

I followed him up the stairs, thinking over a lot of things, from the offhand way that Kyle's mother treated him to the way he had said, "It's just Joanie." Had he really meant it, or did he just want to get her off his back?

His room shouted money. The furniture was all matching, not a hodgepodge of everything nobody else wanted, as my room was. There was a computer on the desk in the corner and a huge stereo with four speakers around the walls. He had a TV on the bookshelf and his own phone.

He pulled two chairs to the desk, and we started work on the play.

He had some great ideas. At first he did the talking and I only suggested funny lines when he asked for them. But after an hour or so of his saying, "Great idea!" and "I like that!" to everything I came up with, I found myself giving my opinion whether or not he asked for it. "I don't think this scene is working right now," I would say, or "There would be more tension if she waited before checking the basement."

Kyle agreed with almost everything, and we got a lot done. Around 9:00 he went downstairs and came up with big bowls of ice cream smothered with fudge topping and M&Ms, and we sat talking while we ate it. The conversation never became personal, though. It was about school and teachers and colleges and the football season. Football naturally led to Danny, and I couldn't resist saying, casually, "I hear Danny's having a party on Friday?"

"Yeah, he is," Kyle said, relaxed and smiling. "It should be great. His folks don't care if he messes up the house, unlike some people I could name. And his neighbors don't care if he makes a noise either. You and Brooke should come. It will be fun."

There, he had said it, just tossed it off as if it were nothing.

"I don't know," I said carefully. "We can't exactly crash if Danny hasn't invited us."

"Are you crazy?" Kyle asked. "Half the school will be there. Besides, I invited you, which is the same as Danny inviting you."

One small voice told me he was just inviting me to be nice, and another argued that he didn't want to come right out and say he wanted me there.

When I saw Brooke the next morning I told her that I had been invited to the party and added, in passing, "Oh, and Kyle says you're welcome to come too, if you want."

"I have to study for SATs on Friday night," she said. "I'm taking them at Palo Alto on Saturday."

"Too bad," I said. "I'll let you know how it went."

"I'm sure everyone will let me know how it went, if you and Kyle get together," she said.

I'd been to a few parties in my life, but none where you could hear the music a block away and couldn't park within three blocks of the house. My mom had lent me her car. Kyle had not offered to pick me up, and I certainly was not going to ask.

"I'll just play it by ear, see how things turn out," I told myself. "At very worst I'll just stay for a few minutes. At best . . . well, who knows."

It took me half an hour of frustrated driving around to find a space, and another half hour to maneuver into it. When I got to the party it was already in full swing. The front door was open, so I let myself in. Every inch of house was packed with people. Kids were sitting on the stairs, spilling out of the kitchen, and coming in a steady stream out of the living room and dining room. I stood in the hallway, looking around for someone I knew well enough to talk to, but I only saw football players and cheerleaders who had probably never noticed my existence.

I was tempted to creep out again and just forget the whole thing. Then Kyle came out of one of the downstairs rooms and saw me. "Hi, Joanie!" he yelled. "You got a drink yet? The drinks are in the kitchen. Come on."

Red-faced and feeling very visible, I pushed my way through the hall crowd to follow Kyle into the kitchen. On the table was a large keg, and Kyle immediately poured himself a beer. I was glad to see that an ice chest nearby contained cans of soda. I took one and opened it. Kyle heard the noise of the tab and looked surprised. "You don't want a beer?" he asked.

"I don't like the taste," I lied, not wanting to say that I didn't drink.

"It grows on you," he said.

"I'm surprised Danny's parents let him have a keg," I said.

Kyle flashed me the famous grin. "Danny's father's been feeding him beer since he was a little kid," Kyle said. "They got the keg for him. They always get us alcohol when we want it. Not like my stuffy parents."

"My parents would freak if they knew I was at a party where alcohol was served," I said.

He looked amused. "They're really old-fashioned," he said. "If you gave a party with no keg, nobody would come."

"Oh, there you are, Kyle," Nicole yelled above the thump of the music and the babble of voices. "We've been looking all over for you. We thought you must have gone upstairs."

She pushed into the kitchen with a couple of other cheerleaders.

"Why would I go upstairs?" Kyle asked, sliding an arm around her shoulders, "if you were down here? There would be no point."

Everyone laughed. Nicole's eyes flirted with him.

I guess I must have put my can down loudly on the Formica surface, because they both looked over at me. "Hey, everyone, you know Joanie?" he said. "She's the one I told you about, who's helping me write this great one-act that's going to win the festival."

"You're so modest, Kyle. That's what I like about you," one of the cheerleaders said.

"I heard Joanie was doing all the writing and you were taking all the credit," Nicole said, turning to me. "Is that true, Joanie?"

"Not true at all," I said. "Kyle's the one who came up with the idea. I'm just helping him with the dialogue."

"Kyle never has trouble coming up with a line," one of the cheerleaders said.

"And you fall for it every time, Sherry," Kyle answered. Again their eyes flirted and I felt insanely, unreasonably jealous. Somehow I kept hoping for a line that never came, something like, "But I've got Joanie now, so you're all out of luck."

Instead the music began again, loud and fast. Sherry grabbed his hand. "Come on, let's dance," she said, and he was swept in an adoring tide of females out of the kitchen. He didn't even look back.

I stayed in the kitchen, sipping my drink and wishing that I hadn't come, or wishing that Brooke were there. "I'll just drink this and go," I told myself a million times, but each time I convinced myself that Kyle might come and find me and ask me to dance with him.

At last I couldn't stand it any longer. I got up and went out the open French doors to the patio.

There was a pool beyond the patio, and the lights from the house danced in the water. It was beautiful and romantic, and I longed to have someone to share it with. I came around the pool and there was Kyle, sitting all alone in the garden swing seat. I looked carefully to make sure first that he wasn't a hallucination and second that he was alone before I said, "Hi, Kyle," in my brightest voice.

He peered at me intently, before he said, "Oh, hi, Joanie."

"Nice night, isn't it?" I said. It was a dumb thing to say, but the only thing I could think of.

"Is it?" he asked. "I don't know. Where is everybody? They've all left me. Poor old Kyle, out here all alone and nobody cares."

"I care," I said.

Kyle patted the seat beside him. "Come and sit next to me, Joanie," he said. "You're a good friend. You understand. You know what it's like."

I didn't know what he was talking about, but I wasn't going to turn down the chance to sit next to him. I sat, not too close but not too far away either. He put an arm around my shoulders. "You know what, Joanie?" he asked. He spoke every word slowly, as if it were an effort to talk. "You're the only friend I've got. The only true friend. Joanie, you understand me, don't you?"

115

"I—I understand," I said, hardly able to believe that this was happening.

"The others don't," he said. "They think I'm always happy. They don't even know. But you know, because you've been through it, too."

I said, "Uh huh," even though I wasn't quite sure what he meant.

"Joanie," he murmured. He leaned toward me. I thought for a moment he was going to kiss me. Then his head dropped onto my shoulder. After a moment or two I realized that he had fallen asleep.

We were still sitting there together, Kyle's head on my shoulder and me not daring to move, when his friends came looking for him much later.

Chapter
Eleven

The warm feeling of Kyle's head on my shoulder, of his voice murmuring, "You're the only true friend I've got, Joanie," stayed with me all weekend. It wasn't just the triumph I felt that Kyle's friends had discovered us together, it was the knowledge that he had chosen me to open up to. I was sure none of the rest of that popular crowd knew that he ever felt lonely or sad. He would never have told them because they wouldn't have understood. But he had sensed right away that I would understand, because I'd been lonely and sad, too. At the time, of course, I had no idea what could possibly make him feel that way, because he seemed to have everything going for him. But I didn't understand about the booze back then, or what his life was like at home. I just felt amazed that we weren't such different people after all.

I couldn't wait to see Brooke's face when she saw us together. She'd finally have to admit that there was something between us, that it wasn't all in my imagination. But on Monday morning it seemed that Kyle had forgotten all about the incident. I passed him in the halls on the way to first period, surrounded as usual by his football friends and hangers-on.

"Hi, Kyle," I called as he was in danger of sweeping past me.

He seemed to notice me for the first time. "Oh, hi, Joanie, how's it going?" he asked, giving me a friendly wave.

"When do you want to get together this week?" I asked. "To work on the play, I mean."

He scratched his head. "Gee, I don't know about this week. We have a big football game on Saturday and the coach is going to work our tails off at practice."

"But we don't have too much time to finish it, do we?" I asked. "You said we should start casting and be in rehearsals by the beginning of November."

"Yeah, I know," he said. "Look, do you think you could go ahead and do some of it without me? I know you could—you're really better at it than I am."

"Sure," I said lightly. "No problem."

"Come on, Kyle. You don't want to be late for Mr. Kalstad. He's already out to get you," Danny said, giving him a nudge.

"You're right. Gotta go," he said. "We'll get together next week and work on the play, okay, Joanie?"

Then they swept by, the royal procession leaving the peasant standing out in the cold. Why did Kyle tell me I was his one true friend then treat me as if I were nobody special? *Maybe he thinks his friends would tease him if he said he liked me,* I thought. *Once we've produced the play and it's a big hit and we win the contest, then he can let everybody see that he cares for me.* Thus comforted I went to my first class.

I didn't see Brooke all morning so I waited beside her locker at lunchtime. She didn't show up until five minutes before the bell for afternoon classes. Then she came rushing up, her arms full of books. It struck me that there was something different about her. She had always taken the trouble to look perfect in every way: the most fashionable clothes, hair shining and neat, makeup just right. I realized that she was wearing the same oversize sweatshirt she had worn on Friday, that her hair looked dull. She had makeup on, but for some reason, it seemed too bright.

"Oh, hi, Joanie," she said.

"Where have you been? I've been waiting for you all period," I said.

"In the library again. I seem to have more work than time."

"Did you skip lunch again?" I asked.

"I had an apple earlier," she said.

"You're going to get sick if you don't eat."

"I'm eating enough. Don't bug me," she said shortly. "I have to get all my work done, don't I?"

She opened her locker, threw her books in, and quickly slammed the door shut again. "So how was the party?" she asked.

"It was fun," I said. "Kyle and I wound up on the porch swing together."

She didn't say anything, so I asked, "How were the SATs?"

"Not so great," she said. "I didn't finish the math section. I'll just have to take them again."

"Are you walking home after school today?" I asked.

"I might go straight to the county library. They don't have the books I need here."

"I'll see you around then," I said.

"Yeah, sure. See you around."

So we parted like two strangers. In the past she

would have asked me to come to the library with her, and I would have gone willingly. At the start of our senior year I had wanted to change things between us, to make our friendship more equal, but something had gone wrong along the way. Now we were drifting further and further apart.

Among the rest of the senior class, my writing the play with Kyle was starting to have an effect. I was suddenly no longer a nonperson, a shadow who followed Brooke around. Nicole passed me in the hall and said, "Hi, Joanie," which seemed like a miracle.

Dereck Johnson, the editor of the school newspaper, stopped me after government class. "So you've been hiding your talents from us," he said. "I hear you're a great comedy writer."

"I don't know about that," I said, laughing with embarrassment.

"That's what Kyle told me," he said. "So how about doing a humor column for the newspaper? We could sure use some lightening up this year. All my writers are so sincere. If I see one more piece about offshore drilling or saving the redwoods, I'll go bananas."

"What sort of thing would you want?" I asked cautiously.

"Whatever you like—you could make fun of teachers, school rules, you name it. It's up to you."

"I'll give it a try," I said, "but I can't promise it will be any good."

"As long as it's not about the environment, I want it," he said. "Next issue goes to press November 15."

I watched him stride down the hall, grinning in amazement that I, Joanie Hammond, had agreed to write for the school newspaper. In one day I had achieved what I had dreamed of for three years.

It was now doubly important that the play be good. I stayed up late at night working on it. I thought about it when I should have been concentrating on trig and chemistry. I listened to people around school and came up with some great dialogue, especially for the cool boyfriend who turns out to be the murderer. By the time I showed it to Kyle, I was pretty happy with it. Kyle read it and was more than happy.

"This is so great," he said. "I'm so glad I got to know you, Joanie. You've really made this whole project. Wait until I show Paul! All we have to do is finish off the last scene and then we can start casting. You will stick around, won't you? We need your input."

"If you want me to," I said, trying to conceal my delight. He still wanted me around. Maybe he really did like me. Maybe he was waiting for the right moment to let me know.

We put up flyers for tryouts the next week. There were six parts: the girl who is in the house alone baby-sitting, her boyfriend, the couple she sits for, the delivery boy, and the gardener. The only really big part was the baby-sitter; she was onstage alone for most of the play. On the morning of tryouts Brooke caught up with me on the way to school.

"So today's the big day, right?" she asked.

I noticed she had taken extra care with her clothes. She was all coordinated in black and white. Usually she looked great in black, but this outfit made her skin look ghostly pale and her eyes look hollow.

"Are you feeling okay?" I asked.

"Why?" she asked defensively.

"You look kind of pale."

"It's almost winter. Everyone looks pale. Anyway, I think I look dramatic, which is perfect for an actress."

"You're going to try out for the play?" I asked.

"I thought I might," she said. "I haven't got anything creative for my application yet."

"Brooke—you already have enough on your application to have it bound in hard cover."

"Yes, but nothing creative," she said. "The lead in a play that won the one-act festival would look good."

"It's a long shot to win the festival," I said

quickly. "None of us really knew what we were doing in the writing department. We know even less about directing."

"I heard it was a really good play," she said, "and a really good part to show off an actress's talent."

She looked at me knowingly. I could read her clearly. She was saying, "I want that part, and you are my best friend so you are going to give it to me, right?"

Thinking about Brooke wanting the lead bugged me all day. Why did she need the lead in a play, for Pete's sake? She had everything in the world on that application, from the social committee to volleyball. She must have realized that she'd make things awkward for me: Everyone knew we were best friends. If she got the part, everyone would say that I helped her get it. Besides, I didn't know if I wanted her to get the part. Right now I was enjoying being the one in the limelight. And yet I could hardly stop her from getting the part if she was good, could I? I'd seen Brooke in plays before. She was a pretty good actress when she wanted to be.

"You want to cast the lead first?" Paul asked me and Kyle that afternoon at tryouts.

Kyle glanced quickly around the room. "I think we'd better," he said, "since there are only two guys here right now for three male parts, and I happen to know that only one of those two can read."

"You set this up, Kyle," Paul said, giving me a wink. "We know you wanted to act in the play yourself. You wanted to be the wicked boyfriend and get to say Joanie's great one-liners, so you persuaded all the other guys not to come."

"Hey, not true," Kyle said. "But seeing that there's nobody here who could do the part as well as me, I might just give it a go."

"Fine. Then Joanie and I will direct and you can act," Paul said. "We've always wanted to boss you around, haven't we, Joanie?"

I could only smile happily, instantly drunk with the knowledge that I was now an official director of the play.

We started calling girls up onto the stage to read the part where the baby-sitter hears someone outside her window. The first girl had a hairstyle about three feet wide and looked like a total airhead. This impression was confirmed when she couldn't get an entire line out without giggling. "Ohmigod! There's somebody out there. I just know there is. I mean . . . whoops, where am I? Lost my place. Sorry." It was clear that she wasn't going to generate much dramatic tension.

The second girl was wearing the shortest miniskirt I have ever seen, combined with the lowest-cut T-shirt. When she crossed the stage she oozed. I saw Paul's and Kyle's eyes pop out of their heads.

When she opened her mouth to talk, she had a high scratchy voice that didn't go with her body at all.

At last we were down to Nicole and Brooke. I thought that Nicole did a better job. She sounded very natural, but Brooke was trying so hard that she sounded forced. We three huddled together in the darkened seats when they had both finished.

"So what do you think, guys?" Kyle asked. "They both did a good job."

"I think Brooke had more feeling," Paul said.

"Yeah, maybe you're right," Kyle agreed. "And she's got more of that helpless look. Nicole always looks like she's in control."

"You don't think Brooke was overacting a bit?" I asked cautiously.

"Maybe right now, but she was trying to impress us," Paul said. "I'm sure we can get that right in rehearsal."

"And you don't think Brooke's voice is a little high?" I asked.

"I think that kind of fits the part, don't you, Kyle? She's supposed to be paranoid by the end of the play."

The two boys nodded. I could see they both wanted Brooke. There was nothing I could say without seeming totally mean.

"Nicole won't mind. She has a million other things to do," Kyle said.

"So does Brooke," I said. "I don't see how she's going to fit rehearsals into her schedule."

"It's only for a month," Kyle said. "Should we announce it right now or post it later?"

"Post it later," Paul said. "That way there won't be any hurt feelings."

So we put up the cast list on the bulletin board the next morning. Brooke came flying over and grabbed me on the way to my first class. "Thank you *so* much," she said. Her eyes were shining and she looked happy for the first time in weeks. "You don't know how much this means to me. You are a true friend, Joanie. I'll always appreciate this."

"It wasn't me," I said. "Paul and Kyle thought you were the best."

She smiled sweetly, as if she didn't believe a word I was saying. "I know I wouldn't have stood a chance against Nicole if you hadn't been there," she said. "She's such good friends with Kyle and Paul. And she's a great actress, too. I know you must have put in a good word for me, and I just wanted to tell you that you're a great friend." She slipped her arm through mine. "We'll have so much fun working on the play together! And it's such a great play. I can't go wrong with a part like that. I bet the play will win, and we'll be rich and famous!" She reached her classroom door and let go of my arm.

"You want to go out after school and celebrate?" she asked. "Frozen yogurt, my treat?"

"Sure," I said, giving her what I hoped was a convincing smile. As I walked away the smile was replaced by a feeling of guilt that I had accepted her thanks when I had actually tried to keep her from getting the part. And the sadness that she had gotten it anyway. She would go back to being Brooke, in the limelight, while I would slip back to being Joanie in the shadows.

Chapter Twelve

I hadn't realized until we started rehearsing the power that a director has to boss people around. I hadn't had the chance to do much bossing around in my life. In fact, apart from one month as blackboard monitor in second grade, I don't think I had done any at all. But after the first couple of rehearsals I found out that I enjoyed it. It was a great feeling to have the actors do exactly what I told them.

And I have to admit that I especially enjoyed it because Brooke was there. For the first time ever she was doing what I told her.

But something strange began to happen to me.

The thrill of being obeyed sort of went to my head. I noticed it after my first chance at solo directing.

We'd been in rehearsal for a week when Paul came running up to me after school. "Look Joanie, I can't make it tonight," he said. "Do you think you can manage without me?"

"I guess so," I said.

"I'm sure you'll do a great job," he said, and left before I could say another word.

So there I was, alone, a lion tamer controlling my cast of wild actors. I had expected to be an assistant to Kyle and Paul, to sit behind them with the clipboard and make little suggestions when they asked me. I had never dreamed that I would end up there alone—the head honcho. I stood outside the door and breathed deeply, arranged my hair, straightened my sweater, and did my Successful Director Walk onto the stage.

"Okay guys, let's try it without scripts today," I said, clapping my hands for attention.

"Where's Paul?" one of the boys asked suspiciously.

"He can't make it today. I'm directing," I said.

"But we can't do it without scripts yet," Brooke said.

"We only have three more weeks before the festival," I said. "You guys have got to learn your lines."

130

"But I have hundreds of lines, Joanie," Brooke said.

"You shouldn't have tried out for the part if you don't have the time to do it well," I said bluntly. "No books. Take it from the top."

I thought it went well. I had to yell at the gardener a couple of times when he forgot to knock on the door, but apart from that we were really getting somewhere. Kyle was great as the cool, flippant bad guy. I hardly had to direct him at all.

As I got together my notes and had the cast put away chairs on the stage at the end of the rehearsal, I was feeling pleased with myself. I had kept my actors in line and made them do what I wanted. We had gotten through the whole play without looking at scripts! *Maybe I have a talent for this,* I thought, as I turned out the auditorium lights and hurried to catch up with Brooke.

"It's going to be great, isn't it?" I said as I caught up with her.

She gave me a long look. "If you can keep the cast from quitting," she said.

"What do you mean?"

"Joanie, you're acting like a bigshot."

"I was only doing what a director is supposed to do," I said.

"I noticed," she said. "But do you have to pick on every little thing we did wrong, make us do it over

131

and over and give us such a hard time about learning our lines?"

"It's got to be perfect in three weeks, Brooke," I said. "You guys won't get it right without me."

"I think it's more than that, Joanie," she said. "I think you *enjoy* bossing people around. After all, it must be the first time in your life you've had the chance."

"If you don't like the way I do things, you can always quit," I said. "Nicole was really good at tryouts. I bet she can learn the lines."

Brooke glared at me, and I saw I had her trapped. She really wanted the part. "I was just trying to warn you, for your own good Joanie," she said. "Don't let your power go to your head, that's all. People don't like being yelled at!"

"Maybe you just don't like the idea of taking orders from me," I said.

We hardly spoke the rest of the way home.

The next morning Kyle and Paul met me as I was going into English class to tell me they couldn't make rehearsals for the rest of the week.

"The coach made it pretty clear that we'd spend the game on the bench if we didn't show up every afternoon," Kyle said.

"He wouldn't do that, would he?" I asked. "He'd bench his star quarterback and risk losing the game?"

"I think he would," Paul said. "He's on Kyle's case right now anyway, because of that little incident in the locker room."

"What incident?"

"Nothing," Kyle said, grinning. "It's not a polite thing to share with ladies." He slipped an arm around my shoulder. "So do you think you can handle rehearsals this week, Joanie?"

"Sure," I said, my face pink with the double happiness of being put in charge and Kyle's arm draped around my shoulder for all the world to see.

"I'll make it up to you, Joanie," Kyle said, looking right into my eyes. He mussed my hair and walked away. I spent all of English with a silly grin on my face.

That afternoon at rehearsal Brooke did not look happy to see me. She looked up from the steps where she was sitting, half hidden under that terrible Harvard sweatshirt. She looked awful. Her hair was stringy and her sweatshirt seemed to be getting bigger and more stretched out. Was this how she thought an actress was supposed to look? I wondered.

"Kyle's not coming again?" she asked.

"He's got football practice," I said. "The coach is going to bench him if he doesn't show up for the rest of the week. Paul, too."

"Great," she said, rolling her eyes.

"Okay, let's get started," I said, clapping my hands. "We'll take it from the top. On stage, Brooke. Raymond, would you read Kyle's lines for us?"

Everyone moved into position and the scene started. We had only gotten through a few lines when Brooke moved across the stage and knocked over a chair."

"Cut!" I yelled. "Brooke, you're supposed to go behind the chair to the window."

"Sorry!" she said. "Someone must have moved it."

I got up to examine the stage. "It's on its mark," I said.

"Let's start over, and this time, try to put some life into it!"

"Okay," she said, biting her lip.

As the rehearsal continued, I began to wonder if Brooke was deliberately trying to annoy me. She knocked over the chair a second time and flubbed her lines again and again.

"Brooke, what's wrong with you?" I demanded. "You know these lines. You knew them yesterday. Why are you getting them wrong now?"

"Maybe because you're putting so much pressure on me," she said. "You make me stop whenever I get going."

"I wouldn't make you stop if you got it right," I

said. "Now let's go from the beginning and concentrate this time."

She didn't say anything, but her face turned red as she took her place.

Was I being deliberately mean to her? I wondered. Was I trying to get even for all those years of doing what she wanted? For all the years of watching her be the best and the prettiest and the most popular?

By the end of the week Brooke was not talking to me outside of rehearsals. When she looked at me, it was the look of a trapped animal, scared and hostile. I told myself that she couldn't handle it now that I was her equal and not her slave. If that was the way she felt, I didn't need her as a friend anymore, I decided.

I thought this would be a moment of triumph for me, but it wasn't. We'd been friends for almost our whole lives. You can't just stop caring about somebody who has been so important to you. I felt sick inside to think our friendship would end like this. It was as if we were both on a roller coaster that had started down the longest drop in the world, and we didn't know when it was going to stop.

I think that I would have tried to make up with her if I hadn't left my clipboard in the auditorium on that Monday evening.

I was walking home from rehearsal and had

gotten as far as the school gate before I realized I had forgotten it. I didn't want to leave it there, in case a janitor threw away all my precious notes, so I went back for it. As I let myself in through the back door the auditorium was dark, and I had to cross a wide, empty area to get to the stage. I found that I was tiptoeing, hugging the wall rather than walking across the middle, stupidly scared of disturbing some unknown presence in the darkness around me. I was about halfway there when I heard a noise. It sounded like a gentle sigh, just loud enough to be heard, but it made my heart jump, and all at once my senses were alert. My eyes were used to the dark by now and I saw that there was somebody up on the stage—a white form against the dark blue curtains. I was scared but I tiptoed closer.

Then the form turned into two people, standing so close together that I had thought they were one. Their arms were wrapped around each other and they were kissing. I recognized Brooke's sweatshirt and Kyle's dark curls. I was so stunned, I just stood there, my heart pounding, the blood singing in my ears. I left my clipboard and tiptoed out the way I had come.

Chapter Thirteen

I don't remember how I got home. I must have run all the way because I was completely out of breath by the time I let myself in the front door. Once I was safely in my room I wanted to cry, but I couldn't. It was as if all the anger inside me was burning up the tears before they could reach my eyes. "She's taken everything I've ever wanted," I said to myself over and over. "She knew how much Kyle meant to me. I almost had him. I'll never forgive her, ever."

I flung myself down on my bed and hoped for sleep to come and blot out the hurt. When I woke the next morning my stomach was growling with hunger, and I had twenty math problems to finish before school. I looked in the mirror and a puffy-eyed, blotchy-faced monster glared back at me.

A night's sleep had done nothing to soothe my anger. If anything it had made it stronger. All the way to school, every step I took reminded me of another painful time that Brooke had gotten the better of me: The solo she got in choir, even though my voice was just as good, the graduation speech from eighth grade, even though the speech I wrote was funnier. And now, as I relived them, it seemed to me that she had done it all deliberately; she had found out what I wanted most and taken it away.

"The time has come," I said dramatically. "I'm not the old timid Joanie anymore. I am the new strong Joanie, director of the plays, columnist for the newspaper. I'll show her." Then I went through all the ways I could get back at her. I'd write a witty column in the school newspaper in which I made fun of her performance in the play, or I'd sabotage the set so that she'd go to sit down on a chair that wouldn't be there and everyone would laugh. I wanted to hurt her so badly. I wanted her to hurt the way I was hurting.

The strange thing was that I didn't want to punish Kyle. It wasn't his fault that Brooke was acting like a total jerk. Flinging herself into my dream guy's arms seemed like just one more way of betraying me—and she had sure come up with plenty of ways. It was hard to believe that we had ever been best friends when all I could feel for her now was anger.

I forced myself to go to the auditorium that afternoon, although I was dreading the thought of having to see them together. Fortunately Kyle wasn't there, but Brooke greeted me with a bright, "Hi, Joanie, how's it going?"

I grunted and pretended to be reading my notes.

"I didn't see you this morning," she said. "You must have left early."

I grunted again. *Don't push me any further,* I thought, *or I may be the first person to commit murder with a clipboard.*

"I've been working on the scene on the stairs," Brooke said. "I think I've finally got it right."

And then it came to me. I had the way to punish her right under my nose. I could break her during rehearsals!

"Great," I said. "Let's start with that scene, okay?"

"Okay," she said.

"Places, everybody," I yelled. "We're going to start with the breaking-in scene. We need Peter for the telephone and Nick at the back door." I gave the nod and Brooke began. She answered the phone, then as she heard the sound of the door opening, ran upstairs in terror.

"Cut!" I yelled. "Not terrified enough, Brooke. For all you know a killer has just broken in. You run upstairs because it's the only place to run. I want to see you running as fast as you can, half falling up those stairs before the killer comes out of the kitchen. From the top. Action."

I let her get to the top of the stairs before I called her back again.

"Just run up the stairs," I said. "You still don't have the scrambling in terror right. Once more."

Brooke looked at me, then ran up the stairs again.

"And once more," I said.

"Joanie, I'll get it right when we do the whole thing," she said, panting heavily. "I just can't get in character right now."

"You wanted the part. I want my play to be just right," I said coldly. "Now, drop the phone and run up the stairs. I mean really run!"

She dropped the phone, took two steps and collapsed on the floor.

"She fainted," someone called from the audience. People ran from all directions.

"She's only hamming it up," I called to them. "She just doesn't want to run up any more stairs."

I hadn't seen Kyle come into the auditorium, but

he reached her first, leaping onto the stage in one spectacular leap. As he lifted her head she opened her eyes. "W-w-what happened?" she asked groggily.

"You fainted," somebody said. Everyone crowded around her. I was the only one who hung back, sure she was still acting, paying me back for all the stairs.

"Are you okay?" Kyle asked. "Do you want us to call the paramedics?"

Brooke attempted to sit up. "I don't know," she said. "I don't know what happened. I feel so weird."

"I'll drive you home," Kyle said. "Then your folks can decide what to do."

"That's so sweet of you, Kyle," Brooke said.

He swept her up into his arms as if she weighed nothing at all. Somebody picked up Brooke's backpack, somebody else got her script, a third person flew ahead to open doors. The whole procession moved out of the auditorium, following Kyle and Brooke, leaving only me behind.

Chapter Fourteen

By the next morning the whole school was buzzing with rumors of Brooke's collapse. I had spent a very tense night at home, ninety-nine percent sure Brooke had staged the whole thing but one percent not; ninety-nine percent determined not to call her but one percent wanting to make sure she was okay. I put a tape in my Walkman and blasted music into my ears in order to keep my thoughts away. I even fell asleep with my earphones blasting, so that not even a whisper that I had made Brooke faint would be allowed into my dreams.

All the way to school I tried to convince myself that Brooke had pretended to faint so that she didn't have to run up any more stairs. And she had managed to get everyone's sympathy at the same time. *She probably did it to hang onto Kyle, too,* I thought to myself. *She wanted his attention. She wanted to turn him against me.*

When I arrived at school the next morning I found the rumors had gotten there ahead of me. Within five minutes several different people had confirmed that not only had she fainted, but she had been taken to the hospital with an incurable disease and Nicole was going to take over her part in the play. The rumors went unchecked because Brooke hadn't come to school, and the story grew with each telling. I sat next to Becky in government and she sent me a note saying, "Joanie, I'm so sorry to hear about Brooke. You must be really upset! Let me know if I can do anything."

When I went into the auditorium after school Kyle and Paul were already there.

"We didn't think you'd show up, but we came by just in case," Kyle said. "Paul thought we should."

"Why wouldn't I show up?"

Paul glanced at Kyle. "Because of Brooke. We can't rehearse without her. She's in every scene."

"I guess not," I said. "We should have gotten an understudy."

"I wonder how long she's going to be out," Paul said. "Did you hear what was wrong with her yet?"

"I didn't," I said.

Kyle shrugged his shoulders. "When I dropped her off at home yesterday her mother said she'd let her rest and take her to the doctor in the morning. She didn't seem to think it was any big thing. Personally I thought it was scary."

"Didn't she call you and tell you how she was feeling, Joanie?" Paul asked.

I shook my head. Clearly nobody had noticed that we'd not only stopped being best friends, but were hardly speaking to each other anymore.

"What should we do?" Paul asked. "She might have mono or something. We don't have much time for someone else to learn the part if Brooke can't come back. We need to get an understudy."

"We've got Sonya and Toya," Kyle said, making Paul splutter with laughter. Neither of our actresses had improved in the small parts we'd given them. Sonya still couldn't remember one complete line, and Toya still sounded like Bugs Bunny.

"I thought the idea was to win the festival, not have everyone laugh at us," Paul said. "Do you think we should see if Nicole could take over?"

I wanted to say, "Yes, go ahead, ask Nicole," but I kept quiet.

"I think we should see how quickly Brooke recovers," Kyle said. "We can't go get someone else behind her back."

He knows, I thought, nodding to myself. *He knows Brooke was only faking. He has to know. He drove her home.*

Then a thought occurred to me. I'd show Brooke I could play her game! With her away, I could do some serious, in-depth rehearsing with Kyle, just the two of us.

"Hey, I've got a great idea," I said. "How about we spend some time on your scenes, Kyle? This would be a great chance to polish them."

I thought he hesitated for a moment. Then he grinned and shook his head. "I'm already perfect" he said. "And you're crazy if you think I'm going to turn down a free afternoon!"

So it looks as if Brooke has won the battle for Kyle after all, I decided as I walked away. I had offered him a chance to be alone with me and he had turned it down. I had given him the perfect opportunity.

I got as far as the auditorium door when he caught up with me.

"Bye, Joanie," he said. "Tell Brooke I hope she's feeling better."

"What?"

He looked at me strangely. "Aren't you going over to her house?"

"Brooke and I aren't exactly getting along at the moment," I said, my face turning red.

"Yeah, I know," he said, "but that doesn't matter now. She's your best friend. I mean, if it were my best friend, I'd be over there spooning in the chicken soup."

"When have you ever fed anybody chicken soup?" Paul asked, catching up with us.

"So is it my fault my friends are never sick?" Kyle asked. "I wrote on your cast when you broke your arm."

"Big deal," Paul said, giving Kyle a friendly punch.

"Do you want a ride over to Brooke's house, Joanie?" Kyle asked.

"It's okay, thanks," I muttered.

I watched them hurry away and tried to make sense of all the nonsense. Did Kyle really think Brooke was sick? Did he really think she was still my best friend? Outside the building, I started walking fast, not in the direction of home but down Maple Drive, past my old elementary school.

So she fainted, I told myself. *So what? I nearly fainted once when I had the flu. No big deal. Nothing to get worried about. And Kyle's wrong if he thinks I'm going to her house. Why should I bother, after the way she's treated me?*

I cut through the playground behind my old elementary school, remembering the feel of sand scrunching under my feet. As kids Brooke and I had played there a lot, hanging upside down on the monkey bars and riding the little merry-go-round until we were so dizzy we couldn't walk straight. I had a sudden urge to ride that merry-go-round again, to feel the wind in my face and to watch the trees and sky spinning crazily above me. But as I came through the redwood trees at the entrance to the park, I saw that the playground was already occupied by a lot of little kids, so I sat on a bench and watched them.

"You don't know how lucky you are," I told them silently. *"Life is simple for you. You go to school, you play, you eat. You never have to worry about relationships. You're either friends or you're enemies. Simple as that. You play with your friends and stay away from your enemies."*

A group of tough-looking little boys ran up from the sandbox and jumped onto the merry-go-round, holding onto it and running to make it go faster. I remembered doing that too, and the excitement of hauling myself on at the last moment. A little girl, probably about kindergarten age, came running over to join the boys. "Let me on, Kevin," she shouted. "Slow down so I can get on."

"No way, Jose," one of the little boys yelled. The others laughed and ran around even faster. The little girl just stood there, looking helpless. Then suddenly a little shape hurled itself at the biggest boy and grabbed him around the waist.

"You let her play, Kevin Brown, or I'm telling," shrieked a high little voice. The shape was a tiny girl, petite and frail as a china doll, but the effect she had on the boys was instantaneous. The big guy, Kevin, tried to shake her off, but she hung on until she had made him stop running.

"Okay, let her on," one of the other boys growled.

The first little girl climbed on, looking pleased with herself. Her defender brushed off her skirt and walked away again as the merry-go-round started turning faster and faster.

Suddenly it was as if I was having a vision. I knew this scene had happened before.

In this vision, I'm five years old, walking home from the Halloween parade at kindergarten, wearing my butterfly costume. I'm halfway between the safety of the school yard and my own street when a gang of big first-graders appear all around me. They are all dressed in horrible masks. They are very tall and very scary.

"Ha ha," they chant. "We're going to get you. We're going to drink your blood!" I'm trapped, and there is no escape. I'm too terrified even to cry out.

Suddenly there is a magic flash of blue and silver.

149

Brooke, the beautiful fairy princess, hurls herself between the vampires and monsters.

"You leave her alone!" she yells, pushing them backwards. "Go away."

And miraculously they do, sniggering and making dumb remarks. I look at Brooke with awe. Her fairy princess costume is rumpled, her crown has slipped to one side, and her beautiful wand is bent at the top, but she grins at me triumphantly, and I grin back.

The moment I had gone through this scene, I had opened a crack that let in all the sad and scary thoughts I had been keeping out. "What if she's really sick?" I asked myself. "What if it's my fault?"

I tried to get up from the bench but my legs felt all shaky. Kyle was right. Brooke was my best friend. If she hadn't come to save me that day in kindergarten, I'd have been devoured by two vampires and a werewolf. She had broken her magic wand defending me, and she hadn't even cared.

My life hadn't been worth a dime before she arrived at school and made me somebody. She'd taken me to parties with her and stuck up for me. I tried to imagine what life would be like without her, and it seemed bleak and gray.

I don't know why we suddenly started to compete, I thought as I began walking in the direction of home. *There is room for more than one star in the world. It doesn't have to be her or me, except with Kyle. And with Kyle, it's up to him to make up his own mind.* The way I was feeling right now, I'd have let her have Kyle, if only she'd get well again.

The moment I got home I called Brooke's house. Her mother answered.

"Oh Joanie, I was waiting for you to call," she said. Brooke obviously hadn't told her anything about what happened. "I know Brooke would love to talk to you, but she's asleep right now."

"Uh . . . how is she?" I managed to ask.

"I really don't know yet," she said. "She just seems very tired. The doctor wants to run some tests. In the meantime he wants her to rest."

I didn't answer, but my head was full of all the possibilities.

"She's going to be out of school for a few days at the least," Brooke's mother went on, "so I wondered if you'd bring her books home. I'm sure you know her locker combination. If not I can ask her for it."

"It's okay. I know it," I said.

"I really appreciate it, Joanie. Brooke can't afford to be without her schoolbooks right now. She can't let things slide right before applying to colleges."

"Maybe she needs a rest," I said.

"She's getting rest," her mother said quickly. "But she can't afford to fall behind."

The next morning I took an extra bag to school and went straight to Brooke's locker. I figured I'd visit her and bring her books at lunchtime. As I opened her locker, the first thing I noticed was the odd smell. It smelled musty, like a room that has been shut up for a long time. I sniffed suspiciously, wrinkling my nose because the smell was strong. I pulled out a couple of books. Behind them a whole lot of lunch bags were crammed together, and I opened one. It had a sandwich that had gone moldy in it and a withered apple. I opened another, then another. My mouth felt dry, and the back of my neck felt prickly. Brooke hadn't been eating her lunch all year! But why had she left the bags stuffed in her locker? Why hadn't she just thrown them away?

Almost as soon as I thought it, I knew the answer. Because she didn't want me or any of her friends to catch her doing it! She didn't want us to know that she wasn't eating. I remembered all those occasions when she had to go to the library to study and had assured me that she had just eaten an apple. No wonder she had fainted at rehearsal. She was starving herself.

Chapter
Fifteen

I stumbled away from Brooke's locker in a daze. Something was very wrong. I was so out of it, I would have pushed right past Kyle if he hadn't grabbed my arm.

"Yo, Joanie!" he said. "How's Brooke doing?"

I wanted to get my thoughts in order before I talked to anyone. And I wasn't sure how much I wanted to share with Kyle, who didn't take many things seriously. So I started babbling. "I didn't get to speak to her because she was sleeping but her mother said the doctor wanted her to rest and he's going to run some tests on her today and she's probably going to be out of school for a while . . ." I was trying to sound normal, not wanting to let anybody in on my scary secret.

Kyle looked me up and down and then asked, "What else?"

"What else? What do you mean?"

"I meant what aren't you telling me?" he said. "Come on, Joanie—you look scared to death! Is there something really wrong? You can tell me."

The hallway was full of kids hurrying to first-period classes, flowing around us as if we were rocks in a stream. I suddenly felt trapped. My stomach felt as if I'd stepped into an elevator shaft with no elevator in it. "I . . . uh . . . don't know what to say, Kyle. I'm just not sure."

He dragged me to one side, out of the tide of students. "Tell you what," he said. "Let's skip first period and go out to breakfast."

"What?" I stared at him open mouthed.

"I said let's go out to breakfast. It's what I always do when I need some peace. I know a great little place."

"B-b-but I've never cut a class in my life," I stammered.

Kyle flashed me his mischievous grin. "So, you can't leave high school without cutting a class. It's a mandatory graduation requirement. If you're caught you can always say you were worried about Brooke and you had to check on her, which is true."

"But I can't eat anything, Kyle," I said. "I'm too upset."

"So? Sit there and watch me eat. At least we can talk in private."

I suddenly felt overwhelmed by the need to talk to someone about everything that had happened. "Okay," I said. "How do we get out of here without being seen?"

"You really have led a pure and innocent life, haven't you?" he asked. "You go to the gym, cut across the track, and there just happens to be a back entrance to the parking lot! Come on, let's go before the bell rings and hall monitors start patrolling."

He took my hand and grinned. "See how easy it is to start on a life of sin?" he said as we ran across the back quad.

When we were safely in his car, we took off, tires squealing. We looked at each other and smiled.

"Where are we going?" I asked.

"Joe's, down by the freeway," Kyle said. "They make the best breakfasts—big crispy country-style home fries and lots of wonderful greasy bacon. I go there a lot—ever since my mother got on the health-food kick and started feeding us bran flakes, raisin bran, oat bran, and bran bran."

"My mom is the old fashioned kind of cook," I said. "We have bacon and sausage and pancakes every weekend."

"I'll have to come to breakfast at your house then," he said. "It's cheaper than eating at Joe's."

"Whenever you like," I said. "Only I warn you, my mother will start matchmaking the moment you walk in the door. Every time my sister Jackie brought home a boy, my mother started writing out the wedding invitations."

"And what happened?" Kyle asked. "Did she get married?"

"No. She escaped to L.A. She's going to school there," I said.

"And what about you?" Kyle asked. "Hasn't she tried matchmaking with your boyfriends, too?"

"I've . . . never brought a boy home yet," I said.

"Playing it safe. Very wise," he said. "Parents are a pain, aren't they? They either want to rule your life or they don't even notice you exist."

"Which are yours?" I asked.

"Mine?" He made a face. "Mine are so busy fighting the cold war that they don't notice me. They're trying to see which one of them will crack first and move out. It's a battle of nerves."

"That's awful, Kyle," I said.

"It's okay. It gives me freedom," he said.

"I suppose that's one good thing," I agreed. "Mine want to know every detail of my life, and Brooke's . . ." I stopped in mid-sentence. For a while I had forgotten why we were escaping from school.

"And Brooke's put too much pressure on her," he finished for me.

"Right," I said. "How did you know?"

"Because she told me," he said. "The other night after rehearsal she got very upset. You'd yelled at her because she hadn't learned her lines, and she was scared she'd never learn them in time. I tried to help her, and suddenly she started crying. I didn't know what to do, so I put my arms around her and . . ."

"And?" I asked. I could feel my cheeks turning red.

"And then she flings her arms around my neck and starts kissing me. Man, was I surprised."

"Oh, so you weren't really . . ." I blurted.

"Weren't really what?"

"Never mind," I said. "So what did you do?"

He laughed easily. "The girl needed comforting, so I was very comforting. She felt much better afterward."

"I see."

"She was embarrassed as hell afterward," he added. "She said she didn't know what had come over her. She said she just needed to cling onto somebody because she was about to crack."

"To crack?"

"Yeah. She said she just couldn't handle everything in her life, but she couldn't drop anything. You know her parents. She told me all about them. They sound like monsters."

"They're not bad," I said. "It's just that Brooke is an only child. She's their entire life. They've put all their dreams into her. They want her to go to Harvard."

"Harvard?" He sounded surprised. "Are her grades good enough for that?"

"I don't think so," I said, "and I think Brooke knows it. That's why she's taken on all this other stuff. She's got this crazy idea in her head that if she does enough, Harvard will be impressed."

"So that's why she's been pushing herself so hard," he said.

Kyle swung the car into a potholed parking lot beside a diner.

"There's one more thing, though," I said slowly. "She hasn't been eating."

"She's on a diet, you mean?"

"More than that, I think. I found her locker full of old food that she'd hidden in the back, as if she'd stuffed it there and wanted to forget about it."

"That's weird," Kyle said. He switched off the engine and we sat in silence. "You think she could be anorexic?"

There. He had put a word to my fear. I nodded. "I think maybe she is," I said.

"Why would she want to go on a diet?" Kyle asked. "She's always looked super skinny to me."

"That's right," I said. "She's never had to worry about her weight like I have. I always envied the way she could wolf down ice cream and not put on a pound. Why would she suddenly want to stop eating?"

Kyle shook his head. "I don't know much about this sort of thing, but I do know that anorexics can starve themselves to death."

"But the doctor will find out, won't he?" I asked, my voice wobbling.

"Maybe not unless she tells him," Kyle said. "And if she's been hiding it from all of us, chances are she'll hide it from the doctor, too. It depends how much weight she's lost."

"So what do you think we should do?" I asked.

"Tell her parents? Make them see what they are doing to her?" he asked.

I shook my head. "I don't want to go behind Brooke's back. I'd better talk to her first. She might not want to see me after all the horrible things I did to her."

"What horrible things?" he asked.

"Never mind. I was mad at her. I didn't realize . . . a lot of things. I didn't realize how much the pressure had gotten to her. I'll talk to her. What she needs right now is a friend."

"You want me to drive you over to her house after breakfast?" he asked.

"She's going for all those tests this morning," I said. "Besides, I'd better not cut any more classes. I don't want to start on a life of crime like yours. I'll go right after school this afternoon."

"Okay," he said, "although the life of crime is fun."

"You know me. Good old sensible Joanie," I said. "I tried to change my image, but I guess you can't change the sort of person you are."

"At least people know where they are with you," he said. "I like that in a person." He pushed open the door, and the smell of frying fat came out powerfully to meet us. "Are you really going to sit there and watch me eat?" he asked.

A waitress went past with two enormous platters of fried eggs, home fries, sausages. "Maybe I'll force down a fry or two," I said, smiling at him. "I wouldn't want you to worry about me not eating, too."

Kyle laughed as he led the way to a corner table.

Chapter
Sixteen

Brooke's mother didn't want to let me in when I showed up on her doorstep that afternoon. She took the bag of books from me, blocking the doorway. "It was very nice of you to bring Brooke her schoolbooks," she said. "I'll tell her you stopped by."

"Is she awake?" I asked. "I'd really like to say hello since I'm here."

"I don't know if it's wise for her to have visitors yet, Joanie," she said. "The doctor says she's very run down and needs a lot of rest."

"I won't stay long," I said.

"We don't know what's wrong with her yet, Joanie. It could be something contagious. We haven't had the test results."

161

I know what's wrong! I wanted to tell her, but I kept a pleasant smile on my face. "I have to see her, Mrs. Stevenson," I said. "It's very important."

She looked at me for what seemed an eternity before she nodded. "All right, just a few minutes, though. She seems to tire so easily."

That's because you've pushed her to the point of starving herself! I wanted to yell, but I smiled politely and followed her into the house. Our house always had that lived-in look. My father's newspaper was often on the coffee table, along with my mother's coffee cup and letters from my sisters. Brooke's house always looked as if it were a page from a catalog. There was never a thing out of place. There were plants where there ought to be plants and just the right book on the coffee table. When we were little, Brooke's mother kept all her furniture covered in plastic and even put a plastic runner along the hall carpet so we couldn't mess anything up. I used to hate sitting on that cold slimy plastic that stuck to my legs. I guess that was one of the reasons that Brooke used to come over to our house all the time in those days.

I tiptoed down the hall to Brooke's bedroom, making sure my shoes left no dirt on the carpet. Brooke's mother opened the door without knocking. "Joanie's here to see you," she said. "She brought your books. I've told her not to stay too long. Do you think you could eat another bowl of chicken soup yet?"

I held my breath for the answer.

"Sure, that would be nice," Brooke said.

Maybe I had been worrying for nothing. Maybe she ate normally at home and just skipped lunch at school.

When I walked into the room I got a shock. Brooke looked so thin and pale, lying propped on her big white pillows, that you could almost see through her. She managed a weak smile. "Hi, Joanie," she said.

"Hi," I said, perching on the end of her bed. "How are you feeling?"

"Still kind of woozy every time I stand up."

"Did they find out anything from the tests?"

"It's not mono," she said, "so that's good, isn't it? The doctor said he thinks I'm just overtired."

I nodded. "That is good."

"You brought my books?"

"Here." I held out the book bag.

"That's nice of you. Did my mom ask you to?"

I nodded. She made a face. "I was sure she wouldn't let me lie here without increasing my vocabulary!" she said. Then something seemed to occur to her. "How did you get in to my locker?"

"I know your combination."

I thought her face started to flush. "That's one

163

good thing about having a best friend, isn't it?" she said. "You know everything."

I nodded. "That's right," I said. I played with the lace edging to her quilt. "Did you tell the doctor you weren't eating?" I asked gently.

"What?"

"I found all those old lunch bags, Brooke," I said. "I put two and two together. Did you tell the doctor you have an eating disorder?"

Her face was deep red now. "I don't have an eating disorder," she said. "I've just skipped a few meals to get my weight down."

"Get your weight down? Brooke, you are the skinniest person I know."

She shook her head firmly. "I used to be," she said. "I put on too much weight last summer. I couldn't seem to get it off again."

"Brooke, you didn't need to lose weight," I said. "You looked just fine."

"But I got to be the same size as you!" she blurted out. We stared at each other.

"Thanks a lot! I worked hard to get down to a size eight!"

"I didn't mean it like that," she said. "You look great. Really great . . . too great."

"What do you mean?" I asked cautiously. "How can I look too great?"

Her blue eyes were so enormous they seemed to

164

take up half her face. "I was always the one people looked at before," she said. "I'd never had to compete with you! I got scared, Joanie."

"Scared of me?"

"More scared of *me* really," Brooke said. "Being good at things used to come so easily. Suddenly I wasn't good at anything anymore. Everything happened at once: My parents started talking constantly about Harvard, asking me about my homework every minute, waving SAT preparation books in my face, and you started overtaking me at the same time."

"Overtaking you?"

"Yes, Joanie. You changed so much. You were always the one person I didn't have to impress or compete with. You were always there—my security blanket. If I didn't get the best solo in choir I could always say to myself, 'at least Joanie's impressed that I got a solo at all.' Then suddenly you showed up after a summer in L.A. and wham! You're looking better than me. When I found out that we wore the same dress size, I started to panic. Then things got even worse. You were going out with Kyle. You were writing the play. Suddenly everywhere I went people were saying, 'Isn't Joanie great? Doesn't she look good this year?' I know I'm not a very nice person, Joanie, but I couldn't handle it. Not on top of everything else."

"It didn't mean you had to stop being a star because I was getting some attention for once," I said.

"I know," she said. "It just seemed like the final prophesy of doom for me. It seemed that I was slipping further and further into failure, and I couldn't stop myself."

"So you started taking it out on me," I said quietly. "Putting me down to make yourself feel better."

"I know," she whispered. "I heard myself saying all those ugly things, but I couldn't seem to stop."

"And I felt so hurt and angry that I started getting back at you."

"Doing what?" she asked innocently.

"Yelling at you in the play. Making you do all those scenes over. Having you run up all those stairs."

"I thought I was really bad!" she exclaimed. "I kept telling myself that everyone else got their parts right the first time, but I was so dumb I had to do mine over and over."

I shook my head. "You weren't any worse than anyone else. I liked the feeling of being able to boss you around for the first time. I guess I'm not a very nice person either."

We were looking at each other without speaking when Brooke's mother came in with a big bowl of chicken soup and some crackers.

166

"Get that down and you'll feel much better," she said.

I saw Brooke shut her eyes as the tray was put in front of her. As soon as her mother shut the door again Brooke put the tray on her bedside table. "Yuck. I really hate chicken soup. She thinks she can solve everything by spooning it down my throat every five minutes."

"Do you eat it?" I asked.

"I throw it out the window," she said. "It's doing that azalea bush good."

She looked at me and we both grinned. Suddenly it was as if a wall of clear ice between us had melted. I moved closer to her on the bed. "So you're not eating at home either?" I asked.

She shook her head and looked down. "I can't," she said. "I started skipping lunch and then breakfast and then suddenly I couldn't eat at all. I mean I physically could not get food down me. It felt as if it was going to stick in my throat and choke me."

"How have you managed so long without your parents finding out?"

"I found excuses to eat at different times from them, or I dropped stuff into my napkin when they weren't looking."

"You're going to have to tell them, Brooke," I said.

"I can't, Joanie. They won't understand. They

don't understand anything. They want me to be perfect. My mother would keep spooning stuff down my throat until she choked me."

"But Brooke you've got to start eating again. Maybe not chicken soup, but something. This is really serious. You can't get over it by yourself."

"I know," she said.

"You have to promise to tell the doctor. I'll come with you if you want," I said.

"Would you? Thanks, Joanie," she said. "It's not going to be easy to talk about this. Everyone will think I'm crazy."

"Everyone will understand that people crack under too much pressure," I said, "or when they put too much pressure on themselves."

"You think they'll understand at school?"

"I'm sure they will," I said. "Right now there are all sorts of interesting rumors flying around about you."

"Really? Like what?"

"That you've got an incurable disease, you'll never walk again."

She grinned. "Sounds dramatic," she said. "And speaking of drama, I guess I can't be in the play anymore."

"You can't?"

"The doctor said I'll be out for at least a couple of weeks. It will probably be more when he finds out I haven't been eating. I don't even know how I'll keep up with my schoolwork, let alone extracurriculars."

"Don't worry about it," I said. "It's no big thing, really. I'm sure we can get someone else to play your part. I'll bring home your work from school every day and try and explain what you missed."

She gave me a beaming smile, just like the old Brooke. "You really are a good friend, Joanie. You've been there for me my whole life!"

I felt a lump come to my throat. "I was just thinking that you've always been there for me," I said. "I'd have been eaten by a couple of monsters if it hadn't been for you."

"What are you talking about?"

"That Halloween when those boys were teasing me and you bent your magic wand defending me, remember?"

Brooke's face lit up. "In kindergarten, you mean? Yeah, I remember."

"We've been friends for a long time," I said.

"I guess I'm glad you found out my secret," Brooke said.

I shook my head. "I'd already remembered those monsters and decided it was my turn to help you," I said. "I'll help you get through this, Brooke, whatever it takes."

She looked down at her quilt, drawing her finger

169

along the lines in the pattern. "Do you think you could help me tell my parents?" she asked. "I don't think I can handle them alone."

"Sure. But this will require some thought," I said. "We have to make them realize that they're putting too much pressure on you. Maybe Kyle can help us talk to them. Kyle's not afraid to talk to anyone."

"Kyle?" Brooke asked. "I don't think I want him to find out."

"He already knows," I said. "I told him about it this morning."

"You told Kyle about my locker? Joanie, how could you!"

"I'm sorry. I needed to tell someone, and he seemed to know something was wrong," I said. "But don't worry. He understands and wants to help you, Brooke. He's a really nice guy."

She nodded. "He was nice to me the other night. He listened while I rambled on and on. Then I started crying."

"I know," I said.

"He told you?"

I nodded.

"I didn't believe it for the longest time, but I guess he does like you," Brooke said.

"As a friend," I said, surprising even myself as I said what I had known all along. "I've been waiting, but we don't seem to be going anywhere. Still, having Kyle as a friend was more than I could have hoped for."

"I was so jealous of you when I thought Kyle liked you more than me," Brooke said.

"But what about Damien?" I asked. "I thought you were crazy about him."

She looked away again. "There isn't any Damien. I mean, he exists, he's a real person. He was at the foundation, but he didn't look at me twice. I just made it up because you talked about guys who liked you. It was all part of the panic. Dumb, right?"

"It's okay. I understand," I said. "I kind of did the same thing with Kyle, pretending that things had gotten much further than they really had. But I was fooling myself about it, too."

"I had a horrible summer," she said quietly. "I hated that job. They treated me like a little kid who was in the way. They only let me do really boring stuff like filing. And you were gone. I felt like I was alone with my parents and all their ambitions. That's why I felt so jealous of you having a great summer in L.A."

There was a silence.

"For best friends we sure kept a lot of stuff hidden from each other, didn't we?" I said at last.

"Let's not do that anymore," Brooke said.

"Fine with me," I said. "It's just not the same when I can't tell you things. I've really missed you."

"Me, too," Brooke said.

Our arms came around each other in a big warm hug. I swallowed back my tears. Brooke wiped her eyes as we drew apart.

"You know what?" she whispered. "I sort of hope I don't get into Harvard after all, so we can go to school together. How am I going survive without you?"

"We'll spend a fortune in phone bills," I said.

"We'll get our own private phone line!"

"Our own fleet of carrier pigeons!"

We started laughing.

"Joanie should be going, Brooke!" Her mother's voice came through the door. Brooke and I looked at each other.

"Quick," she said, "the chicken soup!"

"Okay," I whispered, "But tomorrow I'm sneaking french fries up here." I grabbed the bowl and had just finished tipping it out of the window as Brooke's mother came into the room.

"Oh, good girl. You've finished your soup," Brooke's mother said. Brooke and I looked at one another and had to bite our lips to stop laughing.

"Joanie should be getting home," she said. Then she looked at Brooke critically. "You're looking better than you have in a long time," she said. "Your cheeks are nice and pink for a change. You really have managed to cheer her up, Joanie. That's good. You'll stop by and see her tomorrow, won't you?"

"You bet," I said.

The next evening Kyle came with me to see Brooke's parents. We all sat around the Formica table, Brooke's parents, Brooke, Kyle, and I, and we talked. It was much easier than I thought it was going to be. Kyle did most of the talking and, to my surprise, Brooke's parents listened.

"Is this really how you've felt?" her mother asked, turning to face her daughter.

Brooke nodded.

"Then why didn't you tell us?" her father asked.

"Because you wouldn't let me. The moment I tried to tell you anything you switched straight into your Harvard spiel. I was so scared I'd let you down that I just shut up and tried harder."

"We were doing our best for you," her father said. "We wanted to make sure you got all the chances we never had. Your mother and I will feed you and have you back to strength in no time."

Kyle and Brooke and I exchanged glances. "You don't understand, Mr. Stevenson," Kyle said. "It's not as simple as that. She's going to need to start very slowly with a lot of support and a lot of help."

"Anorexia is a disease, Henry," Brooke's mother said firmly. "People can die from it."

Brooke's father coughed nervously. "So you're telling me that my daughter is dangerously ill, because of us?"

"Not just you, Daddy," Brooke said quietly. "I was putting pressure on myself, too."

"Oh, honey," her father said, and his voice cracked. "We'd never meant to do anything to jeopardize your health. You're so precious to us."

"I know you only wanted the best for me," Brooke said gently, "but maybe I'm not what you think I am. Maybe I'm only ordinary and I'll have to settle for an ordinary school. I won't mind one bit if Joanie is there with me."

She reached across and took my hand. Hers was very cold, and I squeezed it.

"You just do your best, honey," Brooke's father said, "and that will be fine for us."

Brooke's mother nodded. "Let's just concentrate on getting you well again," she said to Brooke. "I'm going to ask Joanie to help look after you and make sure you don't do too much too soon. You'll do that for us, won't you, Joanie?"

I nodded and smiled.

"And you, young man," Brooke's mother said, turning to Kyle, "The girl who winds up with you will certainly be a lucky young woman. You've

174

shown real courage coming and talking to us tonight. You're certainly one in a million!"

I sat beside Kyle in his convertible on the way home and he looked at me seriously. "That went okay, didn't it?"

"It was more than okay. It was like watching a miracle," I said.

"Or a made-for-TV movie," he added.

"You were terrific, Kyle. You said all the right things."

"I think I'll let you treat me to ice cream," he said. "After all, I am one in a million!" And a big smile spread across his face.

"She was right, though," I said as we took off at his usual high speed.

"About what?" he yelled over the noise of the car.

"That the girl who winds up with you will be lucky! I hoped for a while it was going to be me."

He stared straight ahead as he swung the car around a bend without losing speed. "You know my rule, don't you?" he asked.

"Rule?"

"I have this rule never to get seriously involved with a girl at my own school. Not that I've ever gotten seriously involved with anyone! But it's too much of a hassle to date a girl I go to school with. I'd have to eat lunch with her every day and not talk to other girls at parties. And then, when we'd break up it would be awkward."

"Maybe one day you'll meet the right girl and you won't want to break up with her," I said.

"Maybe one day," he said, considering this as if he'd never thought of it before. "But I don't think I'd like to be tied down. I sure don't want to end up like my parents, fighting every day of their lives."

"It could get lonely one day," I said. "When you're old and gray and girls don't swoon at your feet anymore."

"Are you kidding?" he asked, laughing loudly. "I'll be chasing them around the old people's home with my cane! Kyle Carpenter is never going to stop having fun!"

We swung into the parking lot at Baskin Robbins, our tires screeching on the gravel. "So are you treating to ice cream?" he asked.

"Sure," I said.

He turned off the car and put his hand on mine. "Joanie," he said. "If ever I did want to get serious about a girl, I don't think I'd mind being stuck with someone like you," he said softly. "I can be myself with you. I don't have to live up to this image of Kyle who's always laughing, always happy, with no worries. I'd like to know I had a few friends like you around when the going gets rough. Okay?"

"Okay," I said.

Then he took my chin in his hand, pulled me toward him and kissed me gently on the lips.

"Great," he said as he let me go again. "Will you freak out if I order a chocolate-dipped double scoop, with nuts on top?"

There was a big grin on my face all the way to the ice cream parlor. I think Kyle thought I was grinning about the ice cream.

Chapter Seventeen

In the gymnasium the four girls sat silently, each staring at the walls, lost in private memories.

"You probably know the rest," Joanie said at last. "Nicole does, anyway, because she took over Brooke's part in the play."

"What about Brooke?" Becky asked. "She's all right now, isn't she?"

Joanie smiled. "It took a long time and a lot of family therapy," she said, "but she's fine now."

"And what about Harvard?" Gina asked.

"She didn't apply," Joanie said. "The doctor thought it wouldn't be wise for her to be in a stressful situation so far from home. I'm really glad because she's going to U.C. Santa Barbara with me."

"You got into a U.C. campus, Joanie?" Gina asked, surprised.

"Good for you, Joanie," Becky said.

Joanie blushed. "I think it was writing the play that made the difference," she said. "It gave me the confidence to write for the newspaper and a lot of other things, too."

"And what happened with the play?" Gina asked.

"We came in second in the festival," Nicole said. "Wasn't that annoying? We were beaten by this Greek tragedy performed by an all-girls Catholic high school. Weren't they terrible, Joanie?"

Joanie nodded. "They just stood there in gray robes and spoke in these weird monotonous voices. I can't see why the judges gave them first place."

"Probably because they didn't have a clue what was going on, and they didn't want to seem stupid," Nicole said.

"Anyway, second was pretty good," Becky said, "especially for a play you wrote yourselves. I went to see it, and I thought it was very good. Kyle was great, wasn't he?"

"Yes," Joanie said, "Kyle was great."

"I bet he could have become a famous actor," Nicole said.

"He could have been anything he wanted," Becky said.

"Do we have to keep talking like this?" Gina asked abruptly. "We haven't gotten any work done and I have to leave soon."

"Sorry," Nicole said. "I just think it helps to share our feelings."

"How can it help to talk about what Kyle might have been?" Gina demanded. "It's all so stupid and so useless. Now, are we going to get on with decorating ideas or what?"

The other three girls shifted nervously in their seats.

"I guess we should get to work," Nicole said awkwardly.

"I don't think we can do much more today," Becky said. "If we agree on the undersea fantasy theme, let's just get together again with ideas and possible materials at the end of the week."

"That's a good idea," Joanie said. "My dad can probably get us lots of Styrofoam from his factory."

"And I'm going to study up on fish," Becky said.

"Becky! It doesn't have to be biologically accurate!" Nicole exclaimed.

"I didn't mean that," Becky said. "I meant I wanted to have schools of glittery fish suspended from the ceiling so I have to research which fish swim in schools."

181

"You can tell the sort of person who really does belong at Harvard," Nicole said to Joanie.

"I am not going to Harvard!" Becky protested.

"Where then?"

"Yale," Becky said, and laughed along with the others.

"So have we finished discussing?" Gina asked, picking up her things.

"I guess so," Nicole said. "Come up with ideas, suggestions, designs, and, more important, people who can donate materials by Friday, okay?"

They began to walk toward the door. As they reached it Gina said, "Look, I'm sorry I got mad like that. I get so angry when I think about Kyle. It is so, so stupid and wrong. I just can't come to terms with it!"

"I think we all feel like that," Joanie said gently, "but I know I feel better, sharing with you all of my good memories about him."

"And doing something positive like this in his memory," Nicole added.

"I have to get to work, you guys," Gina said, pushing past them to the door. "Some of us won't go to any college at all unless we can pay for it!"

Nicole gave the other two a shrug, and they all followed Gina out of the gym. *If only they knew how I was feeling right now,* Nicole thought. She watched Joanie and Becky go out of the gym together, chatting happily. *Joanie's feeling better already,* Nicole thought. *I wonder if I'll ever find the courage to tell them my story?*

*Here's a sneak preview of Nicole's story from
Senior Year #2:* New Year's Eve

"I wanted to ask you something, Nicole," Kyle said, perching on the end of my bed. "I never got a chance to talk to you alone at school, and you and I don't seem to have coordinating after-school schedules."

"I know," I said. "It's a bummer, isn't it? What did you want to ask me?"

"It's about your party."

"Yeah?"

"We said some things to each other, and you kissed me."

"Uh huh."

"I was surprised," he said. "You weren't acting like yourself. I didn't know how to take it. I still don't. I get one message from you one minute and another message the next. So I wanted to find out once and for all. Did you mean that kiss?"

"Did you?" I asked.

"You know me," he said, laughing. "I'd kiss anything that came into my arms."

"That's what I was afraid of."

"But the thing that surprised me most was not

how you behaved," he said slowly. "It was me. I thought we knew each other really well. I didn't think I had any of those kind of feelings for you."

"And do you?"

"Yeah," he said. "Nicole, I can't stop thinking about you."

"Me too," I said, laughing nervously.

"You can't stop thinking about yourself?" he quipped.

"I'm being serious, Kyle," I said firmly. "I didn't expect to feel anything either. But I did."

"Wow," he said. "This is heavy."

We sat there at opposite ends of my bed, me hugging my knees to my chest, Kyle with his arms wrapped around the bedpost.

"You know me, Nicole," he said at last. "I'm not exactly famous for my long-term relationships. And I've always made it a policy not to get involved with any girl from our school. You remember what happened when we were freshmen, don't you? I dated Delia Hanson, and she went into hysterics when I broke up with her. She went to the principal's office and flung herself on the floor. . . . I swore never again!"

I looked at him and smiled. He still had that little boy's face and that incredible charm. "So what you're saying," I began slowly, "is that you don't think we should get involved. You think it's better if we just forget about that kiss and stay friends, right?" I was trying to be mature by not letting him see my disappointment.

"What I'm trying to say, Nicole," he said, leaning out from the bed as he hung on the pole and swung himself back and forth, "is that I don't know if it would work—you and me, I mean. But do you want to give it a try?"

"I can't think of any girl that would turn you down, Kyle Carpenter," I said.

"Me neither," he said, laughing.

He moved toward me.

"Maybe we should try that kiss again, to make sure it wasn't a fluke," he said. "I mean, we have to make sure we really have something going here, don't we?" As he spoke his lips were moving nearer and nearer to mine. It was a replay of that first kiss, his lips warm on mine, his arms holding me tightly, and all sorts of strange feelings racing up and down my body. When we broke apart I was breathless.